BORDER WAR

Center Point
Large Print

Also by Bradford Scott and available from
Center Point Large Print:

The Slick-Iron Trail
Powder Burn
Outlaw Land

**This Large Print Book carries the
Seal of Approval of N.A.V.H.**

BORDER WAR

A Walt Slade Western

BRADFORD SCOTT

CENTER POINT LARGE PRINT
THORNDIKE, MAINE

This Center Point Large Print edition
is published in the year 2019 by arrangement with
Golden West Literary Agency.

Originally published in the US by Pyramid Books.

The text of this Large Print edition is unabridged.
In other aspects, this book may vary
from the original edition.
Printed in the United States of America
on permanent paper.
Set in 16-point Times New Roman type.

ISBN: 978-1-64358-406-5 (hardcover)
ISBN: 978-1-64358-410-2 (paperback)

The Library of Congress has cataloged this record under
Library of Congress Control Number: 2019946813

BORDER WAR

One

BY THE TREATY of Guadalupe, from El Paso to Brownsville and a bit farther east, the Rio Grande was the boundary between Texas and Mexico. Which was appreciated by the outlaw fraternity. The lawless of two nations evaded pursuit by simply boating, swimming, or wading into another country, leaving the authorities baffled.

Erratic, unpredictable, and unreasonable, "Ol' Debbil River!" Thundering in its sunken gorges, a broad and placid stream across the level rangeland. At times a trickle at El Paso, a roaring flood at Brownsville, spewing six hundred thousand cubic feet a second into the Gulf of Mexico. Or storming against the International Bridge at El Paso and threatening to wash it away, with but a slight flow in its lower reaches. All dependent on the behavior of its tributaries, the Conejos, the Chama, the Conchos, and the Pecos and Devil's Rivers.

The Rio Grande! The Great River! The River of the Palms! Call it what you will, it was and still is a problem, and always will be.

"Yes, Shadow, just about two thousand miles of trouble," Ranger Walt Slade, named *El Halcón*—

The Hawk—by the Mexican *peónes* of the Rio Grande river villages, said to his magnificent black horse. "And we've perambulated ourselves close to the whole length of the darn thing more than once. A blasted nuisance, one would say, but interesting. And the chances are it will be this time, too. So june along, horse; we should make it to Clint by a little after dark, and a chance to put on the nosebag, which we can both use about now. So june along, and stop complaining."

Shadow, who was not complaining, evidently figured there was a possible helping of oats to supplement his recent diet of grass, and quickened his pace a little.

Lounging comfortably in the hull, Slade continued his ride up the verdant Middle Valley, his destination El Paso, situated close to the mouth of the rift in the mountains known as *El Paso del Norte*, The Pass of the North, and near where the westernmost tip of Texas touches the borders of Mexico and New Mexico.

To the north of where he rode, beyond the wide reaches of the rangeland, were the rugged Hueco Mountains, pierced by grim Hueco Pass through which, in the old days, ran the Butterfield Stage Line, California bound. Near at hand were farmlands where grew luxuriant crops—fields of alfalfa, orchards, patches of melons, and other garden produce—with roses, dahlias, and chrysanthemums providing a balance of beauty. Also, vineyards where grew grapes from which the famed golden wine of the Middle Valley was made.

Swaying gracefully to the movements of his great horse, Walt Slade made a picture worth a long day's journey into night to see. Very tall, more than six feet, the breadth of his shoulders and the depth of the chest that slimmed down to a lean, sinewy waist were in keeping with his splendid height.

His face was as arresting as his form. A rather wide mouth, grin-quirked at the corners, modified somewhat the tinge of fierceness evinced by the prominent hawk nose above and the powerful jaw and chin beneath. His pushed-back wide-brimmed "J.B." revealed a broad forehead and crisp, thick hair as black as Shadow's midnight coat.

The sternly handsome countenance was dominated by long, black-lashed eyes of very pale gray, eyes the color of a glacier lake under a stormy sky. Cold, reckless eyes that, nevertheless, always seemed to have gay little devils of laughter lurking in their clear depths. Devils that could, did occasion warrant, leap to the front and be anything but laughing. Then those eyes were "the terrible eyes of *El Halcón*," before which armed and plenty salty individuals had been known to quail.

Slade wore the careless garb of the rangeland—

"levis" as the cowboys called the bibless overalls they favored, soft blue shirt with vivid neckerchief looped at his sinewy throat, well-scuffed half-boots of softly tanned leather, and the broad-brimmed hat, the "rainshed" of the plains. He wore the homely, efficient attire as Richard the Lionheart must have worn armor.

Around his waist were double cartridge belts, from the carefully worked and oiled cut-out holsters of which protruded the plain black butts of heavy guns. And from those big Colt forty-fives his slender, muscular hands seemed never far away.

Shadow was a fit mount for his distinguished master. Full eighteen hands high, his ebony coat was glossy. His eyes were large, full of fire and intelligence. His every line bespoke speed and endurance.

So, under a sky flaming with the many-colored splendor of sunset, rode Walt Slade, Texas Ranger, Captain Jim McNelty's lieutenant and ace undercover man. Rode a trail that had always been an adventure trail and very likely would again.

Slowly the vivid hues faded. In the west a great star glowed and trembled. The lovely blue dusk sifted down from the hilltops. With it came a brooding hush, and soon the land was wreathed with shadows.

But not for long. A broad orange moon rose in

the east, paled to silver, and flooded the scene with ghostly light in which large objects were plainly visible for some distance—small ones also to the eyes of *El Halcón.*

And still quite a ways ahead, a sprinkling of lights, like fallen stars, came into being. The lights, Slade knew, of Clint, a shady little settlement of mostly adobe houses. With hard by the inscrutable Rio Grande.

Suddenly Slade leaned forward in the saddle, peering. Opposite the winking lights of Clint and less than a quarter of a mile north of the trail another light had appeared. A glow, a flicker, a burst of flame that instantly resolved as a big haystack burning briskly. The glare outlined a nearby farmhouse, a barn, and other outbuildings.

"What in blazes!" the ranger exclaimed. "Trail, Shadow, trail!"

The tall black lunged forward and in a moment was going at top speed, snorting his disapproval of the whole *loco* affair. Slade instinctively reached down to make sure his heavy Winchester, a long range special, was smooth in the saddle boot.

Now figures were spewing from the farmhouse, and the light of the blaze revealed something else that intensified Slade's interest.

Riding away from the farmhouse and the burning stack, half a dozen horsemen were speeding toward the trail. At the rate they were going, they would strike the trail no great distance ahead of where he would be riding if Shadow kept up his flying pace. He curbed the big black a little.

"Something strange about all this, feller, and we don't want to go barging into a hornets' nest," he said. "Easy a little more."

As it was, he was perhaps three hundred yards to the rear when the six riders swerved into the trail, heading west. His remarkable eyes sensed the whitish blur of faces turned in his direction, and he was going sideways in the hull when a hand flashed down and up and a gun spurted fire. The slug whined past, close.

With an angry exclamation, he whipped the big Winchester from the boot, flung it to the front and squeezed the trigger.

A howl of pain echoed the report. He saw an arm fly up and drop helpless. Answering bullets stormed past. But Shadow, who knew his business, was weaving and slithering in a weird dance, his rider ducking and swerving.

The Winchester spoke again. There was another howl; a leg flopped crazily. Then the discomfited sextet whisked around a bend in the trail and out of sight. Slade slowed his mount still more. Shadow could easily overtake them, but it wouldn't be the smart thing to do; they could hole up and wait for him, with the advantage all theirs.

He glanced toward the haystack, which was swiftly burning down. Men were dashing water onto the roof and against the side of the barn, which was too close to the stack for comfort. He hesitated a moment, then swerved Shadow from the trail and into the streets of Clint. Riding up to the site of the conflagration might also be not exactly wise. Looked very much like a case of arson, and the thoroughly irritated farmers might be in a mood to whack any head that showed. He had noted that the six riders wore cowhand garb much like his own, which might well be not the best calling card, circumstances being what they were. He'd hear all about it in Clint, sooner or later. He headed for the prosperous *cantina* owned by one Tomas Cardena, who also boasted the title of Mayor of Clint.

Two

THERE WERE PEOPLE in the streets now, exclaiming, gesticulating, gazing toward the fire, in which their attention was too absorbed to give the lone horseman any thought.

Plump, jovial, and efficient Cardena was standing in front of his *cantina*, from where he had an excellent view of the conflagration, when Slade drew rein at the hitchrack. He stared incredulously, let out a joyous whoop.

"*Capitán*! Is it really you, or do my old eyes deceive me?"

"Guess they're not making any mistake," Slade replied smilingly. Old *amigos*, they shook hands with warmth.

"That you should so soon return I did not hope," said Cardena.

"Got here rather sooner than I thought I would when I left," Slade replied. "Nice to be back, even though the section is still a trouble spot."

"And the *caballo*, ha! He me remembers," Cardena chuckled as he stroked Shadow's glossy neck. "The horse of the one man who lets none touch him without his master's approval, but his friends he does not forget. To my barn we will

14

take him, where all his needs will be cared for. Then back to the *cantina* and a feast fit to the day. Come, *Capitán*."

"Tomas, what's the meaning of that?" Slade asked, gesturing to the haystack, which had now burned down to little more than a smolder, without setting fire to anything else. Cardena shrugged.

"The farmers the cattlemen will blame," he said.

"Feuding again, eh?" Slade remarked.

"So it would seem, *Capitán*," Cardena answered. "Some here, more so nearer El Paso. Haystacks burned, shots fired over the heads of workers in the fields, cattle stolen. And each blaming the other."

"And quite probably leaving the field wide open for an organized outfit of real owlhoots," Slade observed. "Same old story."

"And with *Capitán* here, the same old ending," Cardena said cheerfully as he pounded on the stable door.

"Hope you're right," Slade smiled.

"Was I ever wrong?" the *cantina* owner asked. "Open, sluggard, open!"

The door swung open to reveal the old Mexican keeper, a sawed-off ten-gauge shotgun in his hand. He, too, instantly recognized both Slade and his horse and had a hearty greeting for both, plus a deep bow for *El Halcón*.

Knowing that Shadow would lack for nothing, Slade and Cardena returned to the *cantina*. Seating Slade at a table near the dance floor, the owner hurried to the kitchen to make sure a repast commensurate to the occasion would be prepared without delay. The old cook stuck his head out the door, waved a greeting, bowed, and disappeared like a jack-in-the-box. A few minutes, and Cardena rejoined Slade.

"Sheriff Serby is—how would *Capitán* say it—fit to be the tied hog," Cardena chuckled.

Slade laughed at the way Tomas' mission-taught English phrased it, but reflected that Trevis Serby's letter to Captain McNelty intimated that the lanky old peace officer really was fit to be hogtied.

"But he will the better feel now," Cardena predicted. "Ha! Of the golden wine from the Middle Valley grapes *Capitán* will partake, *si*?"

"Yes, I think I will," Slade accepted. "Lays a good foundation for the sort of prime surrounding your kitchen boys are throwing together."

"They feel, as do I, that to serve *El Halcón* is the honor great," Cardena said.

"*Gracias*," Slade rejoined soberly, appreciating to the full the high compliment paid him. Cardena sipped his wine and abruptly asked the question Slade knew he had been itching to ask all along but had refrained from in hope that he, Slade, would broach the subject.

"I heard guns shoot. Did *Capitán* fire?"

Slade told him precisely what happened on the trail.

"And you wounded two?"

"Yes," Slade answered. "I didn't shoot to kill, for I was not just sure what it was all about, and a law enforcement officer must be sure. And incidentally, I believe they unwittingly played into my hands by trying to kill me, and gave me something to work with. Suppose some of the farmers from up there will be dropping in here later?"

"It is most likely," Cardena replied, shooting him a curious glance. However, *El Halcón* did not elaborate on his remark and addressed himself to the really excellent repast that was being set before him. He had finished eating and was enjoying an after-dinner cigarette and a final cup of steaming coffee when half a dozen men entered, making their way to the bar. Their dress proclaimed them farmers.

They were sober-appearing men approaching middle age, with a couple of exceptions. All had keen eyes, and their bearing was assured.

"The *hombre* large and the older is Eph Prescott, whose stack was burned," Cardena remarked. "This way he looks."

"So do the others," Slade said. "I've a notion they'll be coming over shortly."

Slade was right. After sampling his drink and

speaking a few words with his companions, big old Eph Prescott disengaged himself from the group and approached Slade's table.

"Son," he said, "was sorta far to see by moonlight, but it strikes me you were the feller who had the gun-fightin' with those devils who burned my stack."

"We were not exactly throwing kisses at one another," Slade conceded. Prescott rasped his square chin with a horny forefinger.

"You look like you be a cowboy," he remarked.

"I have been," Slade admitted.

"And those fellers who burned the stack looked to be cowboys, too," Prescott rumbled pointedly.

"Yes, they did," Slade agreed. "And they undoubtedly saw that I was also dressed as a cowhand and rode like one. Have a chair, Mr. Prescott—I believe that's your name—I wish to have a little talk with you."

Prescott hesitated, then sat down, regarding the ranger expectantly. Slade let the full force of his cold eyes rest on the farmer's face. Prescott fidgeted under that bleak stare.

"I gather, Mr. Prescott," Slade said at length, "I gather you blame the cattlemen of the section for the off-color things that have been happening hereabouts, right?"

"If not them, who?" Prescott countered defensively.

"Remains to be seen," Slade replied. "Mr.

Prescott, doesn't it seem a little strange that cattlemen, as you judge were those who set fire to your haystack, who must have surmised as you did that I was a cowhand, would have endeavored to kill me?"

Prescott again rasped his chin, and mumbled something unintelligible.

"Wouldn't it be more reasonable to believe that they, judging me a cowhand, would have concluded that I was bent on a similar errand and instead of throwing lead at me would have welcomed my advent on the scene?" Slade pursued inexorably. Prescott hemmed and hawed, his gaze shifting uneasily. Then abruptly his eyes met Slade's squarely.

"Son," he said, "the way you put it, it does 'pear sorta reasonable. But what about the ranchers sayin' us fellers steal their cows and run 'em across the river? We don't do any such thing."

"I know very well you don't," was Slade's instant rejoinder. "And," he added grimly, "I'm going to make it my business to see that the ranchers also know it. This sort of thing has happened in the section before—seems folks will never learn—and right here is an example of what takes place when honest men get to feuding, each blaming the other for everything off-color that happens, and giving the outlaws a free hand to operate to their advantage."

"Beginning to think you have the right of it,"

Prescott said. "I'm going over to the bar to talk with the boys."

Cardena speculated his broad back and remarked sententiously, "When *El Halcón* speaks, those with ears to hear listen."

"I really believe I may have instilled doubt in his mind, which is something," Slade said. "And I've a notion the others will string along with him."

"Of the farmers he is the head *hombre*," Cardena nodded. "I think *Capitán* the good night's work did, all told—wounded two *ladrónes*, set the farmers to thinking, as will the cattlemen when he them approaches."

Meanwhile Prescott had engaged the bartender in conversation.

"Pete," he asked, "who is that young feller I was talking to, and what is he?"

"That's Mr. Walt Slade, Sheriff Serby's special deputy, when he's in this section—does a lot of moving about. The Mexican boys call him *El Halcón*," the drink juggler replied.

"*El Halcón*," the farmer repeated. "Seems to me I've heard that before."

"Quite a lot of folks have heard it, and will hear it again," the bartender said dryly. "Believe you have a Mexican cook, haven't you, Mr. Prescott? Ask him to tell you about *El Halcón*; may surprise you some."

Another farmer spoke up. "Seems I've heard it

said that the feller they call *El Halcón* is sort of an outlaw himself."

"The world's full of blankety-blank idjuts who'd do well to tighten the *látigos* on their jaws," snorted Pete. Old Eph Prescott registered approval.

"Can't see Tomas Cardena takin' up with no outlaws," he observed.

Owing to his habit of working alone as much as possible, and often not revealing his ranger connections, Walt Slade had acquired a peculiar dual reputation. Those like Sheriff Trevis Serby, who knew the truth, maintained vigorously that he was not only the most fearless but also the ablest of the rangers. While others, who knew him only as *El Halcón* with killings to his credit, were wont to declare just as vigorously that he was himself but an owlhoot too smart to get caught, so far.

But others of this group were his stanch defenders, pointing out that he always worked on the side of law and order, often with law-enforcement officers, such as Serby, of impeccable repute who welcomed his assistance when the going got rough.

"Killings to his credit? You're darn right to his credit! Anybody he ever killed had a killing overdue. We could sure use a lot more like him. An owlhoot? Don't make me laugh!"

So the argument would rage, with Slade going

his carefree way as *El Halcón*, well satisfied with the present, and apprehensive of the future not at all. And treasuring most what was said by the Mexican *peónes* and other humble people:

"*El Halcón*! The good, the just, the compassionate. The friend of the lowly, and of all who know sorrow, or trouble, or persecution. May *El Dios* ever guard him!"

The deception worried Captain McNelty, the famed Commander of the Border Battalion of the Texas Rangers, who feared his lieutenant and ace-man might come to harm because of it but was forced to admit that it opened up avenues of information that would be closed to a known ranger, and that outlaws, thinking him just one of their own brand, sometimes grew careless, to their grief.

At the bar, Eph Prescott remarked, "Come to think of it, I've heard it said that *El Halcón* is just about the best shot in Texas. Well, after seeing him puncture those two devils at about four hundred yards by moonlight, I'm ready to amble along with that."

"The singingest man in the whole Southwest, with the fastest gunhand," said Pete the barkeep. "Gents, you can figure it right on both counts."

Cardena glanced at the clock over the back bar and spoke to Slade. "Surely *Capitán* intends not to ride to El Paso tonight; it is late."

"I'd planned to, but things didn't work out exactly as I had figured them to," Slade said, "And, as you say, it is late. Guess I'll wait until morning. It has been a long day and little sleep last night."

"To my *casa* you go; you have slept there before," Cardena said with decision. "My cook will your breakfast get whenever you desire it. Sleep long, and sleep soundly. Lay you down to pleasant dreams."

"*Gracias*," Slade replied. "I'll sure take advantage of your hospitality very shortly. Right now I hanker for another cup of coffee."

"Coming up," said Cardena, "and by the way, I'll send one of the boys to tell my *criados* to wait up for you and let you in. Quite likely they are still up—sometimes I think they never sleep—but we'll make sure."

He beckoned to a swamper who was puttering about nearby and called instructions. The swamper hurried out to bear the word to the servants at Cardena's commodious *casa*, which sat at the edge of a grove that very nearly enveloped it on three sides, the front facing the street being clear. Cardena moved to the back room, his head bartender having called for stock, for although it was late, the *cantina* was still doing plenty of business. Sipping his coffee, Slade studied the patrons.

It was a cosmopolitan gathering. In addition to

the farmers, and others who were undoubtedly town people, there were sprightly young *vaqueros* from south of the Rio Grande and a fair sprinkling of Texas cowhands, Cardena always having been a favorite with the range riders. Also, a few individuals who wore rangeland dress but who Slade shrewdly suspected had not recently known the feel of rope or branding iron in their hands. They kept to themselves and conversed one to another in low tones.

The cowboys regarded somewhat askance the tight group of farmers and began clumping together. But as they caught fragments of the conversation between Slade and the grangers, their expressions changed to something approaching bewilderment, and they glanced to one another in the manner of men who didn't know just what to think.

Which pleased *El Halcón*. Let the leaven work; now, he believed, the cowhands also were beginning to wonder a little and experience twinges of doubt. The seed planted in their minds might well bear fruit.

The swamper returned from delivering Cardena's message to his servants. He nodded to Slade.

"All is in order, *Capitán*," he said. "They await your pleasure."

"*Gracias*," Slade replied. "I'll move along as soon as I finish my coffee."

"*Buenas noches, Capitán,*" said the swamper, bowing low.

The crowd was thinning, for it was really quite late. Eph Prescott and his companions stopped on their way out to shake hands again with Slade and wish him well. A few minutes later, several of the cowboys also departed. They slowed as they passed *El Halcón*'s table, hesitated. One spoke up.

"Good huntin' to you, Mr. Slade, and hope to see you again soon," he said.

"You will," Slade promised smilingly. "We'll have a little gabfest together before long." The punchers grinned and bobbed, and headed for the swinging doors. Slade glanced around, missed several other faces. He waved to Cardena with whom he would talk again the following day, and sauntered out.

Three

IT WAS A PLEASANT NIGHT and Slade walked slowly, pretty well satisfied with developments so far. He felt he had gotten somewhere with both the farmers and the cattlemen of the section. Farther west, he knew he would encounter less difficulty, for there he was known and was well acquainted with the ranchers and many of the farmers.

The situation was far from being unique. Always there was a certain amount of friction between the grangers and the ranchers, the ranchers maintaining that the farmers had taken over what had always been open range and should have remained open range, the farmers accusing the ranchers of trying to hog everything, especially the bottom lands which with irrigation produced fine crops but were no good for cows. More than once and in more places than one, Walt Slade had ironed out differences and persuaded the rivals to live together amicably to the advantage of both. Here and for several miles to the west and east to nearly the Malone Mountains, the farmers were, comparatively speaking, newcomers. Which complicated matters. However, Slade was optimistic as to the future. He dismissed the problem from his mind for the moment and turned his attention to more immediate matters.

For as he strolled along the deserted and mostly dark streets, for no good reason he could put his finger on, he began to grow uneasy.

In men who ride much alone with danger a constant stirrup companion, there births and grows a subtle sixth sense that warns of peril when none, apparently, is near. And in *El Halcón* that sense was highly developed. He slowed his pace still more and began giving close heed to his surroundings.

Abruptly he realized that after the farmers had held his attention for a few minutes, the three individuals in rangeland garb but whom he had catalogued as not working cowhands and whom he had been studying during the evening were among the "missing" faces when he glanced around the room after Prescott and his companions passed through the swinging doors.

"May have meant nothing, but blast it! Somehow I don't feel right about it," he told a friendly lamppost under which he was passing. "A hunch? Well, hunches have paid off in the past."

Indeed, the voiceless monitor of the unexplainable sixth sense was setting up a clamor in his brain, a warning he had learned not to ignore.

"Anyhow, I'm not going to walk up to

Cardena's front door, with a street light right before it, until I sorta scout things and get the lowdown on what's in the wind," he concluded.

Putting the resolution into effect, he turned a couple of corners and approached the *casa* by way of the grove that flanked it on the south. It was very dark under the trees and there was considerable underbrush, so he felt sure he would not be spotted as he crept cautiously toward the walk that led from the street to the house. He reached the final straggle of brush and dimly saw the shadowy forms of the two drygulchers gazing toward the walk. A murmur of voices reached his keen ears.

"Shoot soon as he shows, don't take chances, he's bad."

Slade smiled grimly. He had the devils dead to rights. Everything was working out fine. Another slow step, hands gripping the butts of his big Colts. Yes, he was all set.

But not even *El Halcón* could anticipate the vagaries of a pig. One, a big one, was sleeping in the grove, at the edge of the growth. Slade's forward-questing foot came down squarely on its paunch.

A sky-splitting squeal! A wild flurry and scramble! Slade was thrown off balance and out into the light of the street lamp.

"It's him!" barked a voice. "Shoot! Shoot!"

It is debatable if the pig tried to make amends,

but as it made a wild dash to get away from there, it barged squarely into Slade and knocked him flat, the utterly unexpected suddenness of the move nullifying the outlaws' momentary advantage. Lead screeched over the prostrate ranger's body as the outlaw guns blazed. He rolled sideways, whipped out his guns, and shot with both hands, again, and still again.

Answering slugs came close. One ripped the sleeve of his shirt, another the leg of his overalls. He fired as fast as he could squeeze trigger, heard a gasping cry, then a hollow moan and a thud of something falling. He sent bullets whizzing toward the sounds.

Abruptly he realized no more lead was coming in his direction. Thumbs hooked over the cocked hammers, he peered and listened. There was no further sound from the outlaws, and he could just make out two motionless forms on the ground. Very cautiously, his eyes never leaving the two prostrate forms, he eased erect. Still no movement. He began ejecting the spent shells from his Colts and replacing them with fresh cartridges.

There was turmoil inside the *casa*, lights flashing up. The front door banged open to reveal Enrique, Cardena's major-domo, a cocked sawed-off shotgun in his hands.

"*Capitán*!" he shouted. "All is well with you?"

"Fine as frog hair," Slade called back. "Come take a look."

Enrique approached, the shotgun trained on the still forms. "Shall not I make sure, Capitán?" he asked suggestively.

"Really, I don't think it is necessary," Slade replied smilingly. "I believe I got them both dead center. Didn't look so good for a moment, though." He and Enrique scanned the dead faces. Slade at once recognized them as two of the nondescript individuals who had attracted his attention in the *cantina*.

Now people attracted by the shooting were approaching, cautiously. Slade waved them to come on.

"And send somebody to fetch Cardena," he said to the major-domo.

Enrique spoke to the *criados*, who were edging in close. One hurried off to care for the chore.

Quickly, quite a number of the curious were grouped around the bodies, peering, exclaiming, questioning. Several recognized Slade and called him by name. In answer to the questions, he explained exactly what happened, stressing the part played by the somnolent *puerco*, which was received with chuckles and laughter.

Cardena arrived, with him a couple of swampers and several of the kitchen help.

"Figured the boys would be needed to pack the carcasses to the barn," he said. "Want me to send a wire to Sheriff Serby at El Paso?"

"Yes, a good idea to do so," Slade replied. "He'll want to look things over."

"I'll take care of it," said Cardena. "I'll rouse up the operator. So the devils didn't waste any time trying to even the score, eh?"

"Either that or I was recognized as *El Halcón*, I'd say," Slade answered.

"One or the other, chances are," Cardena agreed. "Doesn't matter, so long as it didn't work. And if I can locate that pig, I'll see to it he lives out a life of plenty. Now what?"

"Now I'm going to bed," Slade replied. "Will examine that pair more closely after I rest up a bit. Beginning to really feel the need of a spell of ear pounding."

In a comfortable bed, Slade slept soundly until well past midmorning, arising much refreshed after the first real night's rest he had enjoyed for some days. Descending the stairs he was met by a smiling young Mexican who proceeded to serve him an excellent breakfast.

After eating, he was sitting in the spacious living room with a cigarette and a cup of fragrant coffee when lean, lanky, and composed Sheriff Trevis Serby strolled in.

"Well, how are you, Walt?" he said as they shook hands. "Got Cardena's wire urging me to amble down here pronto, that you were awaiting me. Knew darn well you must have gotten mixed up in something. The boys over at the *cantina* told me where to find the carcasses. Looked 'em over; ornery-appearing sidewinders. Nothing on 'em of any significance, so far as I could ascertain, 'cept quite a passel of *dinero*. More money than they ever tied onto swinging a rope and a branding iron. Figure it's been quite a while since they did an honest day's work."

"That was my conclusion from the looks of their hands," Slade replied. "About the same brand we have gone up against in this section before. And will again, the chances are."

"Well, the bunch, if it is an organized bunch, got a little taste of what it means to run up against *El Halcón*," the sheriff said. "Yep, the same old story, and with the same old ending; on that I'll bet a hatful of pesos."

"Thanks for your confidence," Slade smiled. "Hope you are right."

"I ain't in the habit of being wrong," said the sheriff. "By the way, Cardena is lending us a light wagon and a driver to pack the carcasses to town. That little jigger is okay. Don't come any better."

"You can emphasize that," Slade answered. "Texas born, as were his father and grandfather. But of almost pure Spanish blood. An excellent example of Mexican courtliness and Texas vigor, a combination hard to beat. Speaks both Spanish and English fluently and colloquially, but with every now and then a mission-taught jumble of the words that is a mite startling."

"Yes, he's all right. A good man in a ruckus, too. Plenty of stringy muscle beneath that plump-appearing exterior, and he's active as a cricket. Doesn't often have to call on his floor men to keep order when the going gets rough, as it does in his place now and then."

At that moment, Cardena came down the stairs, stifling a yawn with one plump hand.

"Hello, Trevis," he greeted. "Never a dull moment when *Capitán* is around."

"You can say that about three times," Serby snorted. "Goodbye to peace and quiet."

"Hasn't been too quiet nor too peaceful of late," Cardena pointed out. "Maybe the change will be for the better."

"Eventually it will," the sheriff conceded. "But there'll be plenty of heck raising first. Mark my word."

"Doubtless," Cardena said, accepting a glass of wine from a *criado* to hold him until his breakfast was prepared, which didn't take long.

After he finished eating, Slade and the sheriff enjoyed a cigarette and a final cup of coffee with him, then bade him goodbye for the present and repaired to the stable, where they found the light wagon hitched, the blanketed bodies reposing in the bed. Without delay they cinched up and headed for El Paso, curious glances following them through the streets. Reaching the trail, they speeded up a bit, the wagon horses being fresh and not heavily burdened.

"Should make it before sundown," Serby observed. "That is if nothing cuts loose on the way."

Slade thought it unlikely that an attempt would be made against them in the bright and sunny afternoon, but nevertheless he was watchful and alert. He experienced an unpleasant premonition that they were up against a shrewd and ruthless bunch, the sort that had been plaguing the section of late. Get rid of one such and up crops another. Best to take no chances.

Serby glanced back at the rumbling wagon. "Cardena's boys are scouting around for the horses that pair rode," he remarked. "They'll find 'em, and Cardena'll take care of them."

"And he's sure got an eye out for that pig that knocked me over at just the right time," Slade laughed. "Says it saved my life. Very likely it did, after very nearly handing me my comeuppance by slamming me out of the brush and into the light. Sorta evened the score, though." Serby chuckled and they rode on.

The miles rolled back under the horses' irons. Larger and more distinct rose the bare craggy peaks of the Franklin Mountains, with El Paso spreading out fan-shaped directly under the crumbling face of Comanche Peak. The Sierra Madre range, across the river in Mexico, formed an effective background for El Paso's sister city of Juarez on the south shore.

Soon they were within three to four miles of the city. They rounded a brush-grown curve and Slade reined in staring, with an exclamation of astonishment.

Four

AND WITH GOOD REASON. The river that formerly ran close to the trail wasn't there anymore. Staring ahead some thousand yards, he saw that the stream swerved abruptly from its south-by-east course to due south to roar down a slope and continue south for perhaps seven hundred yards before curving southeast again and gradually resuming its southeasterly course close to the trail.

And in the great bow thus formed were hundreds of acres of prime farming land that had been in Mexico before the river's amazing change of course but were now north of the Rio Grande, *in Texas!*

"What in blazes!" wondered the astounded ranger. The sheriff shook with laughter.

"Didn't tell you about it, 'cause I wanted to see your look when you saw it," he said. "Happened about a month back. We had one lulu of a thunderstorm one night. You know we get some wild ones hereabouts at this time of the year. Remember how the south bank of the river was a rather high ridge? Evidently a lightning bolt, a big one, hit that ridge and tore a big hole in it.

The water rushed through the gap, of course, and quickly widened it and rolled on down to where the land slope changed and shunted it back to where it belonged. That is what must have happened."

"Never heard tell of the like," Slade replied, shaking his head.

"Well, there it is," said Serby, adding sententiously, "and because of it, we've got another Chamizal Zone on our hands, a bad one, worse than the El Paso one. The Mexicans are hopping mad, and you can't overly blame them. They swear all that land belongs to Mexico. Of course, with the River now to the south of it, Texas and the Land Office say it is Texas State Land. Yes, another Chamizal Zone."

The Chamizal Zone, embracing a part of South El Paso and the acreage extending eastward to Cordova Island, contained about six hundred acres. An international dispute over the section was based on controversy regarding the cause of the river's changed course, which put the land in Texas. Many years would pass before the dispute would be settled in Mexico's favor. Meanwhile bad feeling had been engendered from time to time between El Paso and Juarez because of the dispute. Neither really needed the land, but there was a matter of national pride involved. Slade had been largely instrumental in resolving one such controversy to the satisfaction of both parties.

They rode on. But where the river made its abrupt turn and rushed down the slope, Slade again drew rein. Serby gestured toward the quite a few little adobes and cabins dotting the farmland that had been Mexico.

"Lucky there weren't any shacks in line with the breakthrough, or there would very likely have been some drownings," he remarked.

"Yes, the lightning picked a strategic point to strike," Slade agreed thoughtfully. "So that the stream, following its new bed, skirted the farmlands instead of overflowing them. Interesting. Yes, another Chamizal Zone."

"And to complicate things more," said Serby, "somebody has already filed with the Land Office, made a down payment, and got a purchase option on the land and will be all set to take over once the Land Office clears the tract. Must have worked fast, whoever he is, for I happen to know several gents who got something of the same notion but found they were a mite late."

"All this must have happened shortly after I was here the last time, not much more than a month back," Slade observed, still thoughtful.

"You'd been gone less than two weeks," Serby replied. "Fact is, you were hardly out of sight before hell of one sort or another cut loose, with the blasted thunderstorm topping it off. Incidentally, what happened here played right into the hands of the wideloopers. You'll notice that in places over there the river is quite shallow, and broader than it used to be. The hellions took advantage of it without delay. Some of those little Mexican farmers over there know me and came to tell me about it. They said they were sure cows were being driven across the river. They didn't mix into it, of course, knowing better, but just watched. I know they gave me the straight of it because they came to ask me to try and help them from losing their land. I promised I'd do what I could. Maybe you'll be able to do something. Happen to know they think of you mighty well over at the Land Office."

"We'll see," Slade answered, still studying the breakthrough. "Well, guess we'd better amble along."

"Right," agreed Serby. "Getting time to put on the nosebag, and I'm beginning to feel lank."

They continued on their way. The blazing splendor of the sunset was washing the crags of the Franklins with molten gold. The mighty shoulders of the Sierra Madres across the river were swathed in royal purple, their crests ringed about with saffron flame. Beauty and peace, marred only by the evil passions of men. But Walt Slade firmly believed that a new day was dawning for this wild but beautiful land, and that good would ultimately triumph. He rode on in a contented frame of mind.

Another half-hour found them traversing the

outskirts of the town, heading for the sheriff's office on Campbell Street. Several persons recognized Slade and called greetings, which he returned.

Taking their cue from past *El Halcón* performances, these individuals at once surmised what the wagon bore, and the equipage had collected quite a following when it pulled up in front of the office, the crowd exclaiming, questioning. Serby's bellow stilled the tumult for the moment.

"All right, some of you work dodgers pack the carcasses inside and put 'em on the floor," he ordered. "Then maybe you can get Slade to tell you what happened."

Slade obliged to the volley of requests, in detail, for he felt the citizens of El Paso should get the lowdown on the situation without delay. He began with the burning of the haystack and his brush with the firebugs on the trail, concluding with the attempted drygulching, not failing to give the pig the credit due it. Which evoked laughter.

"So, looks like we're up against another bunch of scalawags," somebody remarked. "Well, with Mr. Slade on the job they'll be took care of proper, and in a jiffy." To which there was a general and hearty accord.

Slade was not particularly surprised when several members of the crowd, which was steadily augmented by fresh arrivals, felt sure they had seen the pair in town. For he was confident that El Paso, not Clint, was the outlaw headquarters. In Clint, strangers would be noticed, while El Paso, on the other hand, was a "passing-through" point with constant comings and goings, strange faces being the rule rather than the exception and attracting little attention. The same went for Juarez across the river.

"Well, everybody out," said Serby. "We crave something to eat. Come back later if you wish. Deputy Hall will be here and will let you in. Come on, Walt."

The horses were cared for. The Mexican stable keeper remembered Slade and Shadow. He bowed low to the one, stroked the other's neck and led the one-man horse, to whom he had been introduced on other occasions, to a comfortable stall, a rubdown, and a generous helping of oats.

"Shine he will when next you see him, *Capitán*," the keeper promised. Slade knew he would be good as his word.

These matters concluded, Slade and the sheriff betook themselves to a small hotel nearby, where Slade registered for a room in which he deposited his rifle and saddle pouches. Roony's big saloon and restaurant on Texas Street was their next stop, where Slade received a warm welcome from the owner and the help.

Roony proudly led the way to a table near the

dance floor, a table he knew Slade liked because it gave him a clear view of the windows and the swinging doors, and of a good portion of the room as reflected in the back-bar mirror. Roony was a wispy little man whose strength and agility belied his fragile appearance; Slade had seen him jump three feet in the air from a flat-footed start and kick a man in the face. After his guests were seated, with a snort of redeye in front of the sheriff to hold him until the food was prepared, he hurried to the kitchen.

"Don't bother to order," he said over his shoulder. "You know the boys will be dishing up something special for *El Halcón*."

"He's darn right, something special," the sheriff grumbled to Slade. "Eating with you is a calamity—pounds and pounds!"

"I don't think you need worry for a while," Slade smiled, glancing at the old peace officer's angular form, which certainly did not show a noticeable gain in weight. Serby grunted, downed his snort and hammered for a refill. And when the really excellent dinner arrived, he did as full justice to it as did *El Halcón*. Roony shooed Slade's wellwishers away and gave him a chance to enjoy his meal in peace. Afterward he was forced to endure a barrage of compliments, finally escaping on the pretext of thanking the cook for his offering.

In the kitchen he found Cardena's wagon

driver, well-known there and ensconced behind a full plate.

"*Capitán*, we have heard all," chuckled the old cook, gesturing to the grinning driver. "Surely the eye of *El Halcón* sees all, and his hand is sure."

"Don't forget the pig," Slade reminded, which again evoked laughter.

He chatted with the cook and his helpers for a while in fluent Spanish, then left them bowing and smiling.

"And now what?" asked the sheriff when he returned to the table.

"Now I'm going over to my room and clean up a bit," Slade replied. "I'll be back before long."

"I'll be here; that is if something doesn't cut loose and haul me out," Serby said. "Watch your step, I've a notion you ain't overly popular in certain quarters about now."

"I will," the ranger answered carelessly, and took his departure.

Reaching his hotel room without mishap, he bathed and shaved and donned a clean shirt and overalls, then made his way back to the saloon, where the sheriff was smoking the pipe of peace, fortified with a full glass.

"And now," Slade suggested as he sat down, "suppose you give me a fuller and more precise summary of the off-color things that have been happening hereabouts of late. I've a notion there's more besides the widelooping and the stage holdup with the driver killed that you told me about."

"Plenty," growled the sheriff. "I sorta held back till I got it all lined up straight in my mind. The Wide West General Store was burgled, a slick job all right. And McGinty's Bar, another slick one. Both times the hellions cleaned the safe so fast and quiet that nobody knew anything about it until they opened for business the next day. They got night watchmen working now. Figure you'll say a killing will be in order next time."

"Not beyond the realm of possibility," Slade conceded. "Go on."

"The Arcadia Saloon down toward the river on West Main Street was held up right after closing time by some devils who managed to slip in somehow. Bartender who reached for a gun was shot dead. Several holdups on the streets, a feller killed. Trouble across the river in Juarez, too: a couple of killings and a holdup or two. Wouldn't bother my head about them, but the Juarez folks swear the devils came from this side of the river, which don't help."

"No, it certainly does not," Slade agreed. "Well, guess that's enough to start with. Perhaps you can recall another or two, later on."

"Just wait a little and the chances are we'll have a brand new one or two," the sheriff predicted pessimistically. "Say, you didn't waste any time getting here after I wrote McNelty."

"I was just getting ready to leave Laredo, after taking care of a chore there, when I got Captain Jim's wire," Slade explained. "Just two words—'El Paso'—but I knew what it meant."

"That was McNelty, all right," chuckled Serby. "He sure don't waste words."

"So I took a train to Van Horn, with Shadow in a stall car, and rode the rest of the way, so I could sorta get the lowdown on things," Slade added. "Guess it was a good thing I did. Otherwise, if I'd used the train all the way, I'd have missed out on the fun at Clint."

"You and your notions of fun!" snorted the sheriff.

Slade glanced around the crowded room. "Quite a few unfamiliar faces," he remarked.

"Yep, we been getting quite a few of late," said Serby. "Some of 'em figuring to stay. There's one down at the far end of the bar talking to Roony, the big tall jigger. Showed here about a month back, from the Panhandle, I understand. Name's Gaunt, Herman Gaunt. Bought the Rafter H; you'll remember it, just the other side of the Tumbling J, about six miles to the southeast of here. Runs for something better than ten miles to the east and north to the trail from Carlsbad, New Mexico. Was sorta run down, but he's been shaping it up and restocking it. Good cattleman, all right. Seems sorta nice feller, too. Gets along with folks. Roony kinda takes to him, which he don't to everybody."

Slade nodded and studied Herman Gaunt with interest. A fine-looking man, he thought; lean, sinewy type with broad shoulders. His hair was on the yellow side, his complexion the deep bronze of blond coloring much exposed to wind and weather. He had straight features and a thin-lipped mouth. Slade believed his eyes were light blue but could not be sure at that distance.

New arrivals in a section always interested *El Halcón*. Those appearing to be taking up permanent residence more so than the "passing-through" brand. And experience had taught him that they had one thing in common with the passing-through variety; they embodied all sorts. However, until they evinced something worthy of note, his interest was cursory. He quickly dismissed Herman Gaunt from his thoughts.

Five

"NOW WHAT?" asked the sheriff.

"Now," Slade replied, "I think I'll amble over to Pablo Menendez' *cantina* for a little powwow with him. There isn't much happens on either side of the river that Pablo doesn't learn about. Same goes for Gordo Allendes, the Yaqui-Mexican head of Pablo's 'young men' as he calls them, who help him keep order in his place. Gordo is all right, too, and one of my best *amigos*."

"Yep, Gordo is hard to beat," agreed Serby, "as you've got good reason to know. Chances are at this time of night we'll find Pablo in his Juarez place; you'll remember he opened it up not long before you were here the last time and patterned it after his El Paso rumhole. He spends a lot of time there. So does Carmen, his pretty little niece. She rides back and forth from her house on Kansas Street here. She's a big help to him. In fact, as everybody knows, she just about runs both places. As smart as she's pretty. It was Carmen who talked him into branching out and opening the Juarez place. She insists it'll wind up a real money maker."

"She's right," Slade said. "Already this section

47

is acquiring tourist trade and will a lot more before long, and Juarez will be a prime attraction. And folks across the river think mighty well of Pablo, even though he is Texas born and an American citizen by birth. Which of course Carmen is, too."

"You remember Carmen, don't you?" the sheriff asked with elaborate carelessness.

"Yes, I remember her," Slade replied, smilingly. The sheriff chuckled.

"Going to cinch up and ride across?" he asked. Slade shook his head.

"I think I'll walk," he decided. "Not so very far; the *cantina* is close to the bridgehead, like the one on this side of the river, and it's a nice night."

"Okay," said Serby, "let's go."

"You're coming along?"

"I'm not letting you out of my sight until I turn you over to Gordo and his knifemen," the sheriff declared positively. "Tonight *I'm* playing a hunch, a hunch that says those hellions you tangled with in Clint will be out to even the score. I figure the pair you accounted for were just a couple of hired hands and that the big skookum he-wolf of the pack, whoever the devil he is, don't feel overkind toward you about now."

"Hope so," Slade replied cheerfully. "Maybe he'll be mad enough to come looking for me. Which would be all to the good, seeing as I haven't the slightest idea where to look for him."

The sheriff snorted disgustedly, waved to Roony, and led the way to the swinging doors.

Texas Street was even more crowded than the saloon, and as noisy, but hardly as smoky, which was an advantage. Santa Fe Street was a little better, and they enjoyed the walk to the approach of the International Bridge. Soon they saw its spidery loom against the stars. To all appearances it was empty at the moment, which it wouldn't be later on.

Despite the sheriff's pessimistic hunch, they crossed the span without incident, untoward or otherwise.

Around two main streets leading from the bridge was centered Juarez' busy night life. They were lined with saloons, gambling establishments, dance halls, eating places, and curio shops. Time would come, in the not-too-distant future, when the main street, *Calle 16 de Septiembre*, would attract swarms of tourists avid to sample the border town's attractions.

The street always fascinated Slade; it was so utterly Mexico. He led the way slowly through the laughing and chattering crowd until they reached Pablo's *cantina*. Standing just outside the swinging doors was big, jovial Pablo. Talking to him, her back to the approaching pair, was a girl.

She was a rather small girl, but her measurements certainly left nothing to be desired. The street lights struck glints of gold in her luxuriant mop of curly black hair. Her astonishingly big eyes were black, the deep, lustrous black of a forest pool at twilight. Her sweetly turned lips were the vivid red of the hibiscus bloom.

Pablo saw Slade and the sheriff approaching, but his face did not move a muscle as Slade glided forward, hands outstretched. The next thing Miss Carmen Menendez knew, she was high in the air, her short, spangled, dance-floor skirt swirling in every direction, chiefly up. Before her startled screech had really gotten under way, Slade caught her as she came down and whirled her around in his arms. The screech ended in a squeal of sheer delight.

"Darling!" she chattered. "We've been waiting and watching for you. Tomas Cardena's wagon driver told some of Gordo's *amigos* you were here and they hurried across the river to tell us. Oh, but it is wonderful to see you! And so soon! You must have neglected them all terribly this time."

"Neglected who?" With sublime innocence of expression.

"Why, all your beautiful women, of course." Slade favored her with an indignant glare that evoked only a giggle.

"Oh, it doesn't matter," she said. "Just so you always come back to Carmen.

"Hello, Uncle Trevis," she greeted the sheriff. "So you brought him back to me. *Gracias!*"

"Reckon he didn't need much bringing," Serby replied. "Coming across the river tonight was his notion."

"We passed by your little house on Kansas Street," Slade remarked. "The roses are beautiful."

"But lonely," she said softly. "Their little faces always turned toward the trail. But come on in, Gordo is awaiting you."

The place was indeed a replica of Pablo's *cantina* in El Paso. The big room was softly lighted by many wax candles to supplement the hanging lamps. A really good orchestra played muted music. The bar was long and shining, bottles of every shape and color pyramiding the back bar. Bartenders and waiters were spruce and alert. There were tables for gaming, others for leisurely diners, and a long lunch counter, spotlessly clean.

Lounging at the near end of the bar was Gordo Allendes, his dark, savage face softened by a smile that revealed teeth as white and even as Slade's own. He bowed low to *El Halcón* but shook hands with warmth. Old *amigos*, they had shared stirring adventures in the past. Slade knew the knifeman, in whose veins ran the blood of the Spanish *conquistadores* and the blood of the fierce mountain *Indios*, looked forward eagerly to

51

more of the same. His knife was always "thirsty," as he expressed it.

"I'll have to go on the floor now," Carmen said to Slade. "It is a *fiesta* night and we are already busy, and this is nothing to what is to come. I'll be with you 'fore long, though. There are not enough girls to care for all the patrons who wish to dance, but I'll manage to sit out a number or two with you. And perhaps we can actually dance a number together. So don't go gallivanting off somewhere before I get back."

Slade promised not to, and she skipped away to the floor. Pablo led him and the sheriff to a table close to the dance floor and beckoned a waiter.

"First the wine of Pablo's private stock, the golden wine of the Middle Valley grapes," he said. "Then the eye-that-is-red for the *Señor* Sheriff and the coffee for *Capitán*."

Slade glanced at Gordo, who shook his head the merest trifle and sauntered through the swinging doors.

"Going out to scout around a bit," Slade remarked apropos of the departed knifeman. "He doesn't need to be told what we have in mind; he knows."

"Yep, smart as a treeful of owls," the sheriff agreed. "Don't come any smarter. Wine is okay, Pablo. Lays a nice foundation for a snort."

"The snort will up come *pronto*," Pablo promised, and gave instructions to the waiter. "And the snack that is prime?" he insinuated. "Already the cook his stumps stirs."

"Oh, there's no resisting you," Serby sighed. "Bring it on! Bring it on! How about you, Walt?"

"Guess I can risk a small helping, even though it hasn't been overly long since we ate dinner," Slade conceded.

While they were eating, Serby suddenly remarked, "Rec'lect the feller I was telling you about in Roony's? Jigger who bought the Rafter H spread? He just came in."

Slade had already noted the entrance of Herman Gaunt, the tall, lean cattleman Serby had mentioned from the Panhandle country.

Gaunt paused just inside the doors, glanced about as if looking for somebody, spotted the sheriff and waved. Serby returned the salutation. Gaunt found a place at the bar and ordered a drink.

"Yep, seems to be a sorta nice feller," Serby said, and took a sip of his snort.

"Hello!" he exclaimed a moment later. "Looks like a cage must have busted somewhere. Here's another El Paso newcomer just rolled in."

"Who and what is he?" Slade asked.

Serby answered the second question first. "Remember I told you the Arcadia Saloon down by the river was robbed, a bartender shot dead. It shook up old Sam, the owner, pretty badly. Said it could just as easily have been him, and to heck with the liquor business. Said he had all the money he needed and was going back East to enjoy it. Put the place up for sale. The feller who just came in, Chet Wilfred is his name, bought it, and fixed it up quite a bit; pretty nice place now and doing plenty of business. Wilfred had showed up here right after the robbery and let it be known he was on the lookout for a place to invest in. Sam Mumford putting his place on the market came at just the right time for Wilfred."

"I see," Slade replied, regarding Wilfred, who had moved to the far end of the bar and engaged Pablo in conversation. He was not quite as tall as Herman Gaunt, by an inch or two, but looked somewhat heavier, Slade thought. He had a rather rugged countenance with a jutting chin, a prominent nose, and a firm-looking mouth. His eyes were set deep in his head. As to their color, Slade was not sure. Carmen bounced over from the dance floor, and he forgot all about Chet Wilfred.

"I'm starving," she declared. "Haven't had a bite since breakfast. Oh, well, I suppose missing a meal now and then is good for my figure."

"If that's so, I'd say you've been missing quite a few of late," Slade replied, with an appreciative glance. The sheriff nodded emphatic agreement. Carmen wrinkled her pert nose at both of them, and motioned to a waiter who at once headed for the kitchen.

"That's better," she said after some little time had lapsed. "Now I've built up strength to— dance with you, Walt."

"Hmmm!" commented the sheriff. Carmen made a face at him.

"I'll be back as soon as I check stock with the head bartender," she promised. "I see Mr. Wilfred is having another gabfest with Uncle Pablo. He would like to open up a place on this side of the river, or buy one if possible, and wants to know all there is to know about the town's prospects?"

"Well are you going to advise him to establish here?" the sheriff asked.

"Uncle Pablo will advise him," she replied demurely. "What do you think, Walt?"

"I think he would be wise to establish here," Slade said without hesitation.

"I wouldn't think of differing with you," Carmen answered.

"He's as good as opened up, even if he don't know it yet," Serby declared positively. Carmen laughed, and skipped to the far end of the bar. Wilfred bowed courteously and was rewarded with a smile. A few minutes later he departed, Pablo walking to the door with him.

Slade and Carmen had their dance, a couple of them, in fact. Then she returned to the floor for a while. The sheriff joined Pablo at the far end of the bar for a jabber. Gordo Allendes had not yet returned, and Slade was left at the table with his coffee and cigarette, and his thoughts, which were not altogether satisfactory. He absently noticed that Herman Gaunt, the rancher, also was departing.

Six

THE CANTINA was gay and colorful, but Slade was getting restless and just a trifle weary of the smoke and the din, which was more pronounced than usual, fiesta nights making for merriment and noise.

Glancing around the room, he saw that Carmen, Pablo, and the sheriff were all occupied at the moment; he wouldn't be missed for a short while. He stood up and strolled out, breathing deeply of the cool night air.

For some time he strolled about the busy main streets, recognized now and then, returning friendly greetings. Just off the busy thoroughfares and heavily patronized were the cockpits where chicken fighting was as much a national pastime as the bullfight was a holiday spectacle. Slade chuckled and passed them by.

Gradually he worked his way to the corner of Calle Nicolas Bravo where stood the Mission Nuestra Señora Guadalupe De El Paso, which had stood there for hundreds of years. The mission had become the nucleus for the settlement at the Pass.

Slade liked and visited the old church and often

stood in its twilight hush, which was restful to mind and body.

The church had no pews, nor would for years to come, worshippers bringing in serapes, cushions, or small stools on which to sit during services. The interior was the same as it had been when all the worshippers were Indians. Slade smiled as he recalled that legend maintained that each missionary had to keep a bodyguard to prevent his charges from carrying him into the mountains and thus, by his presence, greatly enhancing the prestige of their particular village. Little difference between primitive man and his present-day counterpart.

But now the ancient building knew tranquility and peace, sitting in the shadows with its dreams. Outside, the moon shone brightly, a fragrant breeze whispered. The hum of Juarez' turbulent night life was softened by distance.

Moonlight and peace! Or so it seemed.

Relaxed and refreshed, Slade left the church and walked slowly back toward the *cantina*. He had covered a hundred yards or so when around a corner directly ahead came two men wearing the long, brown, hooded robes of brothers of the order that supported the mission. Walking swiftly, heads bowed, lips muttering, they quickly drew nearer the ranger strolling in the opposite direction. Without a glance they swept past, and as they did so, his amazingly keen hearing caught a sound that would not have been audible to the average ear. A very small and musical sound—the tinkle of a spur. But as he recognized it for what it was and realized its meaning, to *El Halcón* it clanged like a fire bell in the night. He was going sideways and down against a building wall, whipping out both Colts, as the two "brothers" whirled to face him, guns blazing.

Paled by the moonlight, the red flashes gushed back and forth. A slug ripped the crown of Slade's hat. Another shredded his left shirtsleeve, just graining the flesh of his arm. Still a third tore through the right leg of his overalls. Both Colts let go with a rattling crash, and again. Another moment and *El Halcón* lowered the smoking forty-fives and peered through the powder fog at the two motionless forms sprawled on the sidewalk.

He saw exactly what he expected to see. The hooded robes had fallen open to reveal riding boots to which were attached long-necked spurs.

"A very nice try," he remarked to the Colt he was reloading. "Yes, very, very smart, but not quite smart enough. Had they thought to change from rangeland boots to sandals, or had at least removed the spurs, they would have gotten by with it. The little slip! The kind the outlaw brand always makes sooner or later. Just the tinkle of a spur, a sound I figured had no business coming from beneath a brother's robe. A little thing, but it cost them their lives. Well, better be getting away from here."

With a quick glance at the distorted, hard-lined faces, he sped to the near corner and whisked around it as shouts sounded in the distance. The shooting had of course been heard; quite likely somebody would come to investigate, and he did not desire to be pestered with questions at the moment. He turned another corner at top speed, another, and slowed his pace to a stroll, reviewing in his mind the details of the incident.

The way the attempt had been carried out evinced extraordinary shrewdness and careful planning on the part of somebody. Evidently somebody had been keeping tabs on his movements and awaiting a favorable opportunity for a drygulching.

The robe disguise was novel, effective, and had it not been for the little slip of the jingling spur, would have probably been successful. The long, flowing garment effectively hid the rangeland garb the devils wore. Where did the robes come from? Stolen from the vestry where they were kept, no doubt. Perhaps they had been put to other nefarious uses. The brothers were highly respected, and a wearer of a robe would be in a position to learn things.

When he reached the *cantina*, without further mishap, he found Gordo Allendes at the door end of the bar, looking in a decidedly bad temper.

Carmen, Pablo, and the sheriff were at the table: *they* looked expectant.

"Gordo," Slade said, "please see if you can locate the chief of police, the *jefe político*, and bring him here."

"Assuredly, *Capitán*," the knifeman replied, and drifted out. Slade made his way to the table and sat down.

"All right, let's have it," said the sheriff. "Feller came in a little while ago and said he heard shooting somewhere up the street, and from the looks of your hat and shirt, I'd say there's a good chance you know about it."

Without reservation, Slade told them exactly what happened. The sheriff swore under his mustache; Pablo said something in Yaqui. Carmen shuddered.

"I sent Gordo for the *jefe político*," he concluded. "Want him to know the straight of things."

"He's okay," said Serby. "Let us drink."

Quite some time passed before Gordo and the Mexican peace officer appeared. An old *amigo*, he shook hands with Slade, greeted Pablo and the sheriff, and twinkled his eyes at Carmen.

"Sorry am I that so long in coming I was," he said. "But up on Bravo two miscreants who robes of brothers of the order stole it would appear a falling out had, perhaps over the division of the loot, and each other shot dead. So I will report to the *rurales*, the mounted police."

61

"*Gracias*," Slade said, knowing that the chief's version of the affair would relieve him of any possible international entanglement. He presented his own version, as he had to his companions. The old chief nodded his grizzled head. "A chore most excellent, *Capitán*, most excellent," he applauded. "Truly it is said, the eye of *El Halcón* sees all. And his ear hears all," he added with a chuckle. "Would *Capitán* and the *Señor* Sheriff the bodies like to view? I had them placed in my office."

"A good idea," Slade replied. He nodded to Gordo, who had listened without commenting. The knifeman returned the nod and strolled out.

"And while you're gone, I'll go to the dressing room and change," Carmen said. "I'm not going to work any more tonight."

"Hmmm!" said the sheriff.

With the chief leading the way, they repaired to his office to find the bodies of the drygulchers laid out neatly on the floor.

"*Dinero* quite a little in their pockets was," remarked the chief.

"The price of murder, very likely," Slade observed. "It will pay for burying them. Anything else of interest in the pockets?"

"On the table in the corner is all," replied the chief.

What lay on the table were the usual trinkets carried by range riders. They held little interest for Slade. But what did interest him were several small copper cylinders.

"What the devil are they?" asked the sheriff.

"Percussion caps," Slade explained. "With a lighted fuse attached, used to explode dynamite or nitroglycerin."

"What's the hellion doing with such things?" wondered Serby.

"I'd like to know for sure," Slade replied, his eyes thoughtful. "Were there any signs that the devil had worked on a spread recently, it might indicate he used them to blow a waterhole, but the lack of rope or branding iron calluses in his hands show it's been a long, long time since he did an honest day's work. Interesting."

The sheriff looked receptive, but Slade did not elaborate on his remark. He turned to the chief.

"I think that somewhere, at a rack or in a stable, you'll find a couple of unclaimed horses with hats stuffed in their saddle pouches," he said.

"We will search," the chief promised.

Serby glowered at the dead faces. "Ornery lookin' scuts," was his verdict.

"About average, I'd say, perhaps a trifle above the average in intelligence," Slade replied. "I suppose those who saw the bodies immediately concluded they were Texas cowhands."

"I fear so," said the chief. "And they expressed satisfaction that their end was what it was. As *Capitán* knows, some bad feelings exist at the moment, chiefly because of what the *loco* river did by altering its course down to the southeast and creating something like another Chamizal Zone that has caused so much trouble in the past. Perhaps *Capitán* can do something to remedy that, as he has in the past."

"Possibly," Slade conceded. "And referring to another Chamizal Zone, it may end up more in the nature of another Cordova Island."

The sheriff looked puzzled, the chief startled.

Cordova Island was not really an island, but a chunk of Mexico set down in El Paso by reason of an artificial cut made across the Rio Grande; the tract of about four hundred acres remained Mexican territory. Adjoining the Chamizal Zone on the east, it extended as far north as Findley Street, El Paso. Because of its comparative isolation from the rest of Mexico, it had less than one hundred inhabitants, chiefly farmers who grew excellent crops on the rich soil.

Neither the chief nor the sheriff asked any questions relative to Slade's cryptic remark, for both knew *El Halcón* would talk when ready, not before.

"If *Capitán* says all will be well, that is enough," said the former. "Tomorrow with some persons I will speak."

"A good notion," grunted Serby. "Well, reckon there ain't anything else we can do here, and it's late, so I figure we might as well call it a night."

"Which we will do," said the chief. Slade and the sheriff returned to the *cantina*, where Carmen had changed to her riding costume.

"But I'm not riding tonight," she said. "If you two can walk, so can I. Say good night to Uncle Pablo and let's go."

She and the sheriff were watchful as they crossed the bridge and headed for Kansas Street, but Slade gave scant heed to their surroundings, for he knew well that Gordo Allendes and his Yaqui *amigos* with their "thirsty" blades were clearing the way.

"In the moonlight the roses give of their greatest beauty, especially when they are not lonely," Carmen whispered to Slade.

Seven

THE FOLLOWING AFTERNOON, Slade and the sheriff sat in the office, waiting for the coroner to hold an inquest on the bodies of the two Clint drygulchers, and discussing pro and con the situation as it stood.

"And you figure there's some really smart jigger back of the heck raising," Serby observed.

"Definitely," Slade replied. "Somebody with brains and the know-how to use them. Same old problem we have been up against in the past. I've said it so often the repetition is becoming monotonous: we are getting a different type of criminal in the West nowadays. Just as ruthless, just as capable with knife and gun as the old hell-and-blazes brushpopper, but with more brains, more intelligence, often with a better education, and the ability to envisage opportunity, sometimes far beyond widelooping and stage robberies; those being side issues to provide the necessary ready money to hold a bunch together. What's possibly in the works here now may prove to be an outstanding example. I won't be too greatly surprised if it is."

"I don't know what the devil you're talking

about," the sheriff said wearily, "but I suppose you do. You always seem to."

"Well, to put it plainly, all my palaver means that we can look for trouble, and soon."

"And the big chore is to learn who's the brains of the outfit and run him down, eh?"

"Precisely," Slade replied cheerfully. The sheriff gave vent to a disgusted snort.

"Uh-huh, that's all. You make it sound like just running around the corner to fetch a sack of potatoes. Oh, well, Veck Sosna, Juan Covello, and Culebra posed the same sorta problem, and they're pushin' up the daisies. My money's on *El Halcón*."

"Hope you're picking a winner," Slade smiled.

"I am," Serby declared. He glanced out the window. "Here comes Doc Beard and his coroner's jury to set on those two hellions," he announced.

The inquest was brief, allowing that the two drygulchers got exactly what was coming to them and expressing the hope that soon some more of the same brand would be hauled in. Slade was complimented and congratulated. Court adjourned.

The bodies were removed for burial. Slade and the sheriff resumed their discussion, arriving at no satisfactory conclusion.

"But heck, you've only been in the section a couple of days," the sheriff pointed out.

"Not long enough to get a lowdown on things. Although I reckon there's a good chance you've already hit on something you're not ready to talk about. Right?"

"Just a very vague notion about something, sort of in the nature of a hunch, although with something on which to base it," Slade replied.

"So I figured, and your hunches are usually straight ones," said Serby.

"Yes, but a hunch sometimes requires considerable finagling," Slade said. "Well, Gordo and his *amigos* are circulating on both sides of the river and may have something to tell us."

"Darn likely," the sheriff predicted. "Well, while we're waiting, suppose we amble over to Roony's for a snort and a snack. All this palaver makes me hungry, to say nothing of being thirsty."

Slade was agreeable to the suggestion and they set out, walking slowly, enjoying the warm sunshine. But Slade noticed that a cloud bank was creeping slowly up the southeast horizon and that quite likely the sky would be overcast by sunset, the night dark.

Although the hour was still rather early, there was quite a crowd in Roony's. However, Roony had their favorite table reserved, to which he conducted them and beckoned a waiter. The sheriff glanced around.

"See, Herman Gaunt is at the bar," he remarked. "Guess he spent the night in town."

"Probably," Slade conceded. "Not so very far to his spread, though, and he may have returned home last night and then ridden in again this afternoon."

Gaunt evidently noticed their entrance, for he waved to the sheriff. But he made no move to join them.

However, while they were waiting for their order to be filled, somebody did join them, a gentleman in a bad temper. It was old Sime Judson, the Tumbling J owner. He plumped into a chair and glowered at Serby.

"All right, let's have it," said the sheriff. "What's got you all worked up?"

"The same thing that's had me worked up for quite a spell; I'm losing cows," replied Judson. "As you know, last month, not long after Slade left, I lost a hundred head. And just a week ago the hellions took me for better'n another fifty head."

"Sorta late telling me about it, ain't you?" commented Serby.

"What was the sense in botherin' you about it?" Judson retorted. "The critters were gone and you couldn't do anything to get 'em back, and I been busy."

"Any notion where they went?" Slade asked casually, knowing very well what the answer would be.

"Well, that blasted river acting up like it did

and leaving the way to Mexico wide open hasn't helped," Judson replied evasively, adding, "And those Mexican farmers on the land are sorta riled up."

"The threat of losing the land they have owned all their lives, and in some instances owned by their fathers before them, is hardly calculated to fill them with sweetness and light," Slade commented.

"Have to admit you've got something there," Judson said. "Can hardly expect them to do anything to make it hard for the wideloopers, but it don't help us fellers who are losing stock."

"And you are convinced the cows are run across that stretch of farmland?" Slade asked.

"I sure am," Judson declared positively. "We've tried to patrol it and keep a close watch, but somehow the devils slip them by. I reckon the farmers tip them off as to when and where to slide across."

"Okay, we'll try and do something about it," Slade promised.

"And I've a prime notion the hellions ain't going to have it so easy from now on," Judson predicted. "Well, I'll have to be getting home 'fore the devils steal the roof off the house."

He motioned a waiter to serve Slade and the sheriff drinks, and rolled off. Slade watched him through the swinging doors, shook his head.

"I wonder," he remarked, "why people think

that because something appears obvious, it necessarily must be so. I don't know, but they do."

"And what in blazes are *we* going to do about it?" wondered Serby.

"Well, for one thing," Slade replied, "about three hours after dark, you and I, and Gordo if he shows up, and I think he will, and Deputy Hall are going to take a little ride to the southeast."

"You figure the devils are liable to make a move tonight?"

"According to what old Sime said, it's been more than a week since they did," Slade said. "It's a heavily overcast dark night, and the wind is rising. Just the right sort of a night for a little chore of rustling beefs. So I'm playing a hunch that they will hit Judson again, seeing that they appear to have him lined up as they want him. If they do make a move, I figure we have a good chance to hand them a surprise they won't enjoy—and, incidentally, do something to relieve the tension between the farmers and the ranchers, and between El Paso and Juarez. Which would be very much to our advantage. We can do without a Border ruckus to complicate matters, and the situation as it now stands is explosive."

"You're darn right," agreed Serby. "Well, here comes our chuck, and I reckon we'd better get on the outside of it; no telling when we'll get a chance to eat again."

While they were eating, Herman Gaunt

71

sauntered out, waving goodnight to the sheriff, and a few minutes later, Gordo Allendes sauntered in. He was beckoned to the table, served a drink, and informed of what was planned. His black eyes snapped, and his fingers toyed with the haft of the long throwing knife at his belt.

"How's Pablo?" the sheriff asked.

"Fine he is," Gordo replied. "On this side of the river he stays tonight. He and the *Señor* Wilfred talked much of a *cantina* in Juarez Pablo believes will be for sale. When the *Señor* Wilfred from the *cantina* departed, he mounted a *caballo* and rode north. Pablo says he much rides, and thinks that once a *rancho* he may have owned."

"Wouldn't be surprised if he rode a lot," said Serby. "Once a cowman, always a cowman; ain't happy unless he's forkin' a bronk. Right, Walt?"

"Guess you are," Slade agreed smilingly.

Gordo finished his drink and ambled out. Slade and the sheriff relaxed with smokes; they still had quite a bit of time to put in before starting on their ride. Finally Serby knocked out his pipe and glanced at the clock. "I'll mosey over to the office and line up Hall, so he'll have time to eat before we leave," he said. "I'll tell him to meet us at the stable."

Left alone, Slade mentally reviewed the details of his plan. If the outlaws would just obligingly cooperate, he believed it would work. Worth trying, anyhow.

And he believed the outlaws would cooperate. He reasoned that were he a widelooper with an eye on some cow critters, he would regard this black night of wind and threatening rain as providing opportunity.

One of the reasons for Walt Slade's uniform success against the owlhoot brand was his unique ability to put himself in their place, to think as they thought and react accordingly. As Captain McNelty maintained, he not only outfought the owlhoots, he also outthought them.

After a while, the sheriff returned. "I told Hall to meet us at the stable in an hour," he announced. "That about right?"

"Fine," Slade replied. "An hour and we leave."

The hour passed pleasantly enough. They found Hall and Gordo awaiting them. Without delay they cinched up and rode east by south on the river trail.

Slade's prediction that it would be a night of darkness and stormy weather was quickly justified. High in the black heavens the wind wailed, swooped down to earth, flung upward again, eerie, disquieting. The horses snorted nervously and appeared to like it not at all. Nor did their riders, for that matter.

That is, with the exception of Slade, who had to confess that he liked such a night and was thoroughly enjoying the ride with the warring elements for company.

"Witches' weather!" growled the sheriff. "Anything's liable to happen on such a night. Hear that screech? Suppose you'll say it's an owl. Could be, but then again it could be some poor damned soul forced to wander forever through the storm, alone."

The sheriff spoke in jest, and Slade laughed. But he felt the oldtimer was not as comfortable as he might be. The same went for Hall, the deputy, who was not exactly young. Gordo, who feared nothing on the earth or above or below it, merely shrugged and lounged comfortably atop his wiry mustang.

For a while Slade watched the back trail, although he thought there was little danger of them being followed out of town. Finally, no indications of pursuit developing, he faced to the front and concentrated on the darksome vista ahead.

The wan ribbon of the trail unrolled steadily under the churning irons of the horses. The wind wailed and bellowed, with occasional spatterings of rain. The nearby river moaned and muttered, chafing its banks uneasily. The mutter loudened to a rumble as they drew near the point where the stream abruptly changed course to rush down the slope of the ridge. What was now the south bank of the Rio Grande, Slade knew, bristled with a heavy stand of chaparral, but to the north of the former Mexican farmlands, now in Texas, were but scattered clumps of growth and these some distance from the trail. Very likely, he believed, in one of those clumps, Judson's patrolling riders were huddled against the fury of the storm.

"Where do we hole up?" Serby asked.

"Not for quite a ways," Slade replied, and did not elaborate the answer. They rode on passing the thousand yards or so of the farmlands, *El Halcón* not drawing rein.

"Getting pretty well along past the shacks," Serby remarked.

"Guess we are," Slade agreed, and kept on riding. The sheriff grumbled under his mustache but held his peace, for a while. Finally he could hold in no longer.

"We're getting mighty close to where the river turns back to its original course," he said. "Aren't we going to hole up here?"

"No, and not for another mile and a half or so," *El Halcón* replied. "Until we come to a nice thick stand of growth and a ford that cows can easily negotiate with the river as low as it is. Then we'll hole up and await developments."

"You mean the widelooped critters don't get to the river by way of across the farmlands?" Serby demanded.

"That's exactly what I mean," Slade said. "They never did. While Judson and his patrol were concentrating on the farmlands, the rustlers were shoving the herds across the river by way of that ford, with nothing to bother them. As I said this afternoon, it seems folks insist on concentrating on the obvious to the exclusion of all else. That's what's been happening here. So with a little luck we should give the devils a surprise they won't forget for a long time, those that are left to remember. And if we handle the chore properly, there shouldn't be many of this particular contingent left. Beginning to understand?"

"Guess I am," the sheriff admitted wearily. "Anyhow, you always seem to figure things out right. So let 'er blow, high, wide, and handsome!"

Very quickly, they found themselves riding close to the river again. Slade slowed the pace and a little later, with his uncanny instinct for distance and direction, he slowed it still more, until the horses were moving at not much faster than a walk.

"Only a quarter of a mile until we come to the ford, and I want to look things over a bit," he explained. "I don't hanker for it being us getting the surprise."

"You're darn right," the sheriff conceded, glancing nervously around. Gordo muttered something in Yaqui and fingered his knife.

The cloud rack had obligingly thinned somewhat, letting a little moonlight filter through, so that large objects were dimly visible. Plenty of light to enable *El Halcón* to spot the narrow opening in the brush that lined the trail on the river side. He reined in and for moments sat motionless, peering and listening.

"So far, so good," he said. "We're here first, as I figured we would be. We'll ride on past that crack which leads down the bank and to the ford and tether the horses where they'll be out of sight, then pick out a hole-up spot where we can see and not be seen. Chances are we'll be outnumbered, but the element of surprise should be in our favor. Let the cows drift down the bank to the water's edge. The riders will bunch behind them and will be in the light, what there is of it, mounted, while we'll be in the shadow of the brush on foot. I think that should do it, don't you, Trevis?"

"Sounds okay to me," the sheriff agreed. "Suppose we'll have to give the skunks the chance to surrender they very likely won't take."

"We are law enforcement officers and haven't any choice," Slade replied. "Then shoot fast and shoot straight. Let's go!"

He led the way a short distance beyond the opening in the chaparral. The disgusted horses were forced into the growth and tethered securely to tree trunks. Slade dropped Shadow's split reins to the ground.

"This is as close as we dare risk them," he said. "And anyhow the chances are we won't need them in a hurry. Now let's pick our hole-up spot."

He moved toward where the track led down to the level ground and the water's edge.

"This should do it," he said, a few moments later. "From here we'll have a good view of the devils, even though the light will be bad. Now up top the bank and watch."

"Not far from Gaunt's Rafter H," Serby remarked.

"Quite close," Slade conceded.

The sky had brightened still more and the thickets to the north stood out hard and clear.

"Everything plumb peaceful," the sheriff observed cheerfully.

It was, there by the river bank, but not some four miles or so to the north.

Eight

CONCENTRATING on the supposedly off-color doings of the farmers in the course of his talk with Slade and the sheriff, Judson had failed to mention that he had gotten together a shipping herd, well more than a hundred head, to accommodate a buyer with whom he had dealt for years.

Had old Sime mentioned the fact, the coming episode would have been handled differently and with perhaps a more satisfactory ending.

The herd was bedded down around a waterhole with a single hand keeping a watch on the critters to prevent straying. Convinced the widelooped cattle reached the river by way of the farmlands, Judson had not deemed it necessary to post a guard this far east.

During the intermittent showers, the puncher found shelter in a nearby belt of thicket, where he and his mount could keep comparatively dry. Leaning comfortably against the horse's shoulder, he began rolling a cigarette. He half turned at a slight sound behind him.

A crashing blow against the side of his head stretched him senseless on the ground. The tall, bearded individual who dealt the blow bent over him, gun poised for another blow were one needed; it wasn't.

"That takes care of him," the bearded man said to half a dozen other men who clumped around him. "Now we wait for the signal."

By the river bank, the posse lounged at the outer straggle of growth, as comfortable as conditions allowed, gazing to the north. Suddenly the sheriff uttered an exclamation and stared.

Well to the west and slightly north had birthed a glow that quickly climbed the slant of the sky, a bloody refulgence, shimmering, flickering, growing more intense by the second.

"Say, that's right where Judson's ranch house is!" Serby sputtered. "What in blazes! Have the hellions set fire to the *casa*? Sure looks that way." Slade shook his head.

"Burning too fast for the house," he said. "I'd say it's a haystack, a big one."

"There are a coupla big ones not far from the *casa*," Serby recalled. "But why in the blue-blazing heck would they burn a stack?"

"To pull in the patrols if they happen to be farther east than expected," Slade explained. "They'll be hightailing to the ranch house, not knowing what the devil is going on. Very smart! The hellions don't miss a bet and make allowances for everything. They'll be shoving the cows south now, and wasting no time."

The wait that followed was tedious but not too long, for, as Slade predicted, the cows were being shoved fast.

The contrary cloud rack had thickened somewhat again, but there was still light enough for *El Halcón* to spot the moving shadow that was the herd.

"Here they come," he told his companions. "Okay, down into the brush and get set. Should be over one way or another in the next twenty minutes or less."

Tense, alert, the posse crouched at the edge of the growth, with the gray shimmer of the river beyond the narrow stretch of beach, the opening in the chaparral dark and ominous.

Now the peevish bawling of the disgruntled cattle could be heard, growing louder and louder. The thudding of many hoofs became audible, and the click of horses' irons. A few more moments and abruptly the opening in the brush spewed cattle, rumbling, blowing, crowding the narrow beach, thrusting their noses into the water.

Bringing up the rear of the herd bulged seven riders. They halted their mounts on the open space, laughing and talking. At a nudge from Slade, the sheriff's voice rang out:

"Elevate! Up! You're covered! In the name of the law!"

The whitish blur of faces turned toward the

sound, startled exclamations, a clutching of weapons, and the ball was opened!

Weaving, ducking, Slade shot with both hands. His companions' guns boomed in unison. The ranks of the outlaws stormed lead.

But, as Slade planned it, the advantage was with the men on the ground. The outlaw horses, with the terrified cattle milling around and against them, were virtually unmanageable. Their riders fired wildly with little chance to take aim. Two saddles were emptied by the first posse volley. Slade's Colts bellowed and a third horseman hit the ground. The hiss of Gordo's long knife through the air was followed by a gurgling scream. Overhead, the wind howled louder than ever, and down came the rain! A drenching cataract from the black heavens, that blotted out all things. Slade continued to fire in the direction of the outlaws as he heard hoofs pounding the track up the bank, hoping a lucky shot might down a tall, bearded individual he instinctively believed was the leader of the bunch.

Well, if he was, he had evidently escaped, and two of his devils with him, for to attempt to pursue the fugitives would be an act of lunacy, conditions being what they were.

"Quiet!" Slade breathed to his companions and stood straining his ears as he reloaded. He was confident the four on the ground were dead, but best not to take chances. However, he heard no sound of movement. Apparently having decided it had raised enough hell for one night, the elemental uproar ceased as suddenly as it had begun. The rain stopped, the cloud rack thinned and shredded away, letting through a flood of moonlight that revealed four stark forms lying motionless, one with a long knife through the throat. Gordo's thirsty blade was sure!

"Anybody hurt?" Slade asked.

"Hall has a nick in his arm," Serby replied. "Gordo and me didn't get scratched. About you?"

"Another hole in my hat, I guess is all," Slade said.

"Hellions mostly shot over us," Serby remarked. "Yep, you were right; on the ground you got an advantage over the gent forkin' a cayuse."

Slade whistled Shadow, secured his medicants, and quickly had Hall's slight bullet cut padded and bandaged.

"Should hold you till you see the doctor," he said.

"Till I see a bartender," grunted the deputy. "When you patch a feller up there ain't no sense in botherin' Doc, as he'll be the first to tell you."

The cattle had quieted and were nosing the sparse grass that grew near the water's edge. The outlaw horses were nowhere in sight. Very likely, panic stricken, they had followed the others.

"So we'll leave the carcasses where they are

and drive a wagon out to fetch 'em later in the day," said Serby. "Right?"

"A notion," Slade agreed. "Go through their pockets before we leave."

The pockets divulged more than a little money but nothing else Slade believed to be of importance.

"Well, guess we'd better round up the cows and drive them to Judson's *casa*," he said. "Wonder how the devils managed to tie onto such a big herd in so short a time? More than a hundred head. Something funny about this. Okay, let's get going; I'm hungry."

Although it lacked a couple of hours of dawn as they neared the Tumbling J ranch house, the building was lighted, and so was the bunkhouse.

"Reckon settin' fire to the haystack got 'em roused up," Serby hazarded.

But very shortly, after they shoved their bawling charges onto the near pasture, they learned it was more than the burning of the stack that had set the outfit by the ears. The puncher stationed to keep an eye on the shipping herd had recovered consciousness and hightailed to the ranch house to report the theft.

Slade treated the hand's split scalp and decided the injury was not serious but advised the doctor be sent for. Then he proceeded to read Judson a lecture for his carelessness.

"And I think you'll realize that you owe the

Mexican farmers an apology," he concluded.

The subdued and grateful owner admitted it was so. He gestured to the smolder that had been the haystack.

"We'd have swore the farmers set that fire," he added.

"Just as the farmers down at Clint were ready to swear the cattlemen burned their stack," Slade pointed out.

"And I reckon you talked some sense into *their loco* heads," said Judson. Slade smiled, and didn't argue the point.

"And I'm sure indebted to you fellers," Judson continued. "Would have been a heavy loss, nearly a hundred and fifty prime beef critters. The buyer will be expecting them rolled to town tomorrow. Now put your nags into the barn with a surrounding of oats and come on in to breakfast. The cook's stirring his stumps and will have meat on the table in a jiffy."

"Best thing you've said yet," the sheriff declared.

After a hearty meal and a relaxing smoke, the posse headed for town, reaching El Paso shortly after full daylight. The horses were cared for and everybody tumbled into bed.

Nine

WHEN SLADE visited the office shortly past noon, he learned from Deputy Perce Hall that the sheriff and Ron Caldwell, his other deputy, and a couple of specials had already gone to bring in the bodies.

"Trevis told me to take it easy and give my arm a chance," Hall explained. "Really, it's not much more'n a scratch."

"Better be safe than sorry," Slade said. "Did you see Doc McChesney as I told you to?"

"He changed the pad and the bandage and said I'd be okay, that you had taken care of everything. He rode to the Tumbling J to look after that puncher with a cracked head. Said he'd be back before long. And that he expected you to have some more business for him by the time he got back."

"He's an optimist," Slade laughed. Hall chuckled and went to the back room to pour some coffee.

They drank the coffee mostly in silence, for Slade appeared preoccupied and Hall had learned to respect those moods. When the cups were empty, Slade asked a question.

"How long since Trevis and the boys left town?"

"A little better'n an hour, I'd say," Hall replied.

For some moments, Slade studied the clock; then he shifted his gaze to the window, which was bathed in golden sunshine. Abruptly he stood up.

"Perce," he said, "I'm going to ride down and meet them on the way back. If Gordo Allendes shows up while I'm gone and asks for me, tell him I'll meet him at Pablo's *cantina* when I get back, that I don't expect to be gone long."

"Sure for certain," Hall replied cheerfully. "Be seeing you."

Slade headed for Shadow's stable, leaving Hall wondering uneasily if he feared the sheriff might run into trouble on the way back.

A beautiful day of sunshine and warmth had followed the tempestuous night, and Slade enjoyed the ride. So did Shadow, who hated inactivity and snorted gay approval of the chance to stretch his legs. Slade let him set the pace, which was plenty fast. They passed across the Bar A with Sime Judson's Tumbling J following and before long reached the point where the river so abruptly changed course to put a hunk of Mexico in Texas. Here Slade drew rein and sat studying the break in the ridge that had formerly been the south bank.

Studying it with the eye of a trained geologist and engineer, for he was both.

Shortly before the death of his father, which followed financial reverses that entailed the loss of the elder Slade's ranch, young Walt had graduated with high honors from a famous college of engineering. He had expected to take a postgraduate course in special subjects to round out his education and better fit him for the profession he hoped to make his life's work.

This, however, became impossible for the time being and he was sort of at loose ends, undecided just what his next move would be. So when Captain Jim McNelty, with whom he had worked some during summer vacations, suggested that he sign up with the rangers for a while and pursue his studies in spare time, Slade thought the notion a good one.

Long since he had gotten more from private study than he could have hoped for from the postgrad. He was eminently fitted for the profession of engineering and had received offers of lucrative employment from big men of the business and financial world whom he had contacted in the course of his ranger activities.

But meanwhile, ranger work had gotten a strong hold on him, providing as it did so many opportunities for doing good, suppressing evil, helping the deserving, and making the land he loved a better land for the right sort of people. As he had said to himself quite a few times in the course of the years, he was young, plenty of time to be an engineer. He'd stick with the rangers for a while longer.

More than once, his knowledge of engineering had proven of help in consummating his work as a ranger. He was beginning to believe, as he gazed at the tawny flood of the Rio Grande, that here might be still another example.

He rode on slowly, scanning the surface of the slope that dropped gently southward from the trail, his eyes growing more and more thoughtful.

"Shadow," he said at length, "I'm willing to wager that no cows have gone this way and across the farmlands, but horses have. Now what's the answer to that? I'd like to know for sure. Got an idea, a vague one that I'm beginning to believe may straighten out. We'll see."

Turning in the saddle, he gazed long and earnestly toward the grim hills to the north that here were but a moderate distance from the river trail but farther east were nearly forty miles away.

Turning back to face the river, he noted that about two hundred yards out on the farmland, a group was gathering, staring in his direction, evidently talking together with, every now and then, gestures.

Obeying a sudden impulse, he turned Shadow's nose and headed down the slope to the farmlands, riding neither fast nor slow, lounging easily in the hull.

"Hope they don't take a notion to throw some

lead at us," he chuckled to Shadow. "Guess we can risk it," he said, expressing a confidence he did not altogether feel. The Mexican farmers undoubtedly regarded anybody in cowhand garb as an enemy. He had halved the distance when his deep, musical voice rang out, in Spanish.

"Greetings, friends! I trust I am welcome?"

For a moment the ominous silence endured, then suddenly somebody cried, "Brothers! Brothers! It is *El Halcón*!"

A storm of exclamations, heads thrusting forward to peer. Then, as one man, the group bowed low.

"*Capitán*!" called a grizzle-headed old fellow. "*Capitán*! Is it really you, or do our eyes deceive us!"

"Guess they don't," Slade replied smilingly as he reined in beside the group and swung to the ground, hand outstretched.

They crowded around him, shaking hands diffidently but with warmth.

"*Capitán*! This is a day to remember," said the oldster, who Slade correctly surmised was a head *hombre* of the farmers. "*Capitán*, you are needed here. Yes, again is needed the friend of the lowly. Here we have trouble, *Capitán*, but now that *El Halcón* is here, all will be well."

"Thank you for your faith in me," Slade replied soberly. "The trail may be a bit long, but I believe I am safe in predicting that justice will be done."

"If *El Halcón* says it is so, then so it will be," declared the oldster. "Were you riding to join the *Señor* Sheriff, *Capitán*? This way he passed, he and three others, and a wagon. And last night we were sure we heard guns shoot, to the east," he added suggestively.

Slade told them, in detail, what had happened the night before.

"And the ranchers are well on their way to altering their opinions," he concluded. "Tomorrow the *Señor* Judson will ride this way to apologize for misjudging you. Don't shoot him; make him welcome."

The sally was greeted with laughter, and it was promised that old Sime wouldn't eat lead. For a moment, Slade was silent, then abruptly he asked a question.

"*Amigos*, have any of you seen cows being driven across the farmlands to the river?"

"*Capitán*," the old *hombre* answered, "each time there was rain, and the night was very dark. See we did not, but hoofbeats we heard, going toward the river."

A younger man spoke up. "*Capitán*," he said, "one night I out the window looked as the lightning flashed brightly. Horses I got the glimpse of, going toward the river. Cows I saw not. Of course they could have been before the horses; the lightning flash was brief."

"I see," Slade remarked thoughtfully.

"*Capitán*, my adobe is near. Will not you have with me the wine and the—what you call it—the surrounding?"

"I would be honored," Slade replied. "Only have one of the boys keep an eye on the trail and tell me if Sheriff Serby and the wagon put in an appearance; I wish to join him on the way back to town."

"It shall be done," the other stated. "And the oats for the beautiful *caballo*. Come, *Capitán*."

Slade partook of a tasty snack prepared by the head man's wife, a jolly, buxom Mexican lady much younger than her husband. He had finished eating and was enjoying a cigarette and chatting with his hostess when word was called that the sheriff and the wagon had appeared. Slade said *hasta luego* and rode up to the trail. The farmers watched him go. The old *hombre* spoke, in the poetic imagery of *Mexico*:

"Brothers, the dark clouds may gather, but with *El Halcón* here, soon we shall know sunshine again."

"*Ai*! It is so," came the answer. "Where *El Halcón* is, there evil cannot prevail."

Upon sighting Slade, the sheriff spurred ahead of the wagon.

"What the blazes brought you out?" he asked. "Something else cut loose?"

"Hadn't so far when I left town," Slade replied. "Just took a notion to have a gab with my *amigos*, the farmers. We had a very nice talk. Did you do okay?"

"No trouble," said Serby. "We scouted around and made sure there wasn't any trap set and that nobody had tampered with the carcasses, then loaded 'em up and headed for town. Not a bad night, everything considered. Did for four of the devils and got Judson's cows back, and sorta changed his attitude where the farmers are concerned, which helps a lot. And I suppose you took the farmers in tow."

"Judson will be riding down tomorrow to make amends for unjustly accusing them of something off-color; he'll be welcome."

"I don't know how you do it! I don't know how you do it!" the sheriff sighed. Slade smiled, and repeated his conversation with the farmers.

"So they admitted they saw no cattle, just thought they heard the hoof beats of some," he summed up. "Not being overly familiar with cows and the noises they make, they jumped at the conclusion that what they heard was a small bunch of beefs instead of half a dozen horses or so. Which was exactly what the wideloopers wanted them to do."

"Where were those horses headed?" Serby wondered.

"To the river, then they would circle around and regain the trail," Slade replied. "Part of the scheme to cause the ranchers to concentrate on the farmlands and neglect that ford to the east. Simple but effective. Another example of folks thinking the way they wish to think, without giving due regard to the possible and, in this instance, fairly obvious facts."

"Oh, I suppose so," groaned the sheriff. "The way you tell it, it sure makes sense, or seems to."

With the sunset painting the sky in rainbow hues, they reached El Paso, where they quickly picked up a following on the way to the office.

"All right, you work dodgers, lend a hand with the carcasses. Lay 'em out on the floor and have a look. See if you rec'lect anything about the horned toads," the sheriff ordered.

The order was obeyed, the dead faces studied, with several individuals 'lowing they had seen the hellions hanging around town but not quite remembering where and in what connection. Then one of McGinty's bartenders dropped in with something definite to impart.

"Yep, I saw all four of them before," he said. "They were in the place one evening. There was another jigger with them, a big, tall feller with sorta black whiskers. They asked a lot of questions about the town, said it was the first time they'd been here. That they'd been working on a spread over in New Mexico, this side of Carlsbad, the Cross Square."

"There is a spread with that brand, or something mighty close to it, over that way in New

Mexico," the sheriff interpolated. "The Cross Square?"

"Yep, the Cross Square," the drink juggler repeated. "Said they'd like to tie onto a chore of riding hereabouts, sorta liked the looks of the section. Had several drinks and then moseyed out. Civil spoke jiggers, but struck me as being plenty salty."

The barkeep evidently had a flair for the dramatic climax, which he proved by his next remark, spoken slowly and impressively.

"And that night," he said, "was the night the place was busted into, after closing time, and the back room safe cleaned of nigh onto a week's take!"

"The devil you say!" exploded the sheriff.

"Of course I ain't sayin' those fellers did it," the bartender hastened to add. "I just somehow thought it sorta funny, 'specially as I never saw them again, and they'd said they figgered to drop in often while they were in town. Fact is I dropped in at quite a few places myself just to see if I could spot them, but never did."

Serby turned to the ranger. "Well, what do you think, Walt?" he asked.

"As Bob said, there's no proof that these four devils committed the burglary, but being what they are, it's interesting." He turned to the bartender.

"And the fifth member of the bunch visiting

McGinty's was a tall man with a black beard?"

"That's right," replied Bob. "He wasn't as tall as you, Mr. Slade, but he wasn't short, and I reckon you could call his whiskers black." Slade nodded, and gazed thoughtfully out the window.

"And one of the wideloopers who escaped was sorta tall and had whiskers," remarked the sheriff. Slade turned from the window and cast him an amused glance. Serby looked a trifle sheepish.

"Just the same, I can't keep from doing a mite of thinking," he said, adding shrewdly, "and I've a notion you are thinking a bit, too."

Slade repeated what he had said more than once before: "When nobody is suspect, everybody is suspect."

"Perzactly," nodded the sheriff. "So I reckon it's up to us to keep our eyes skun and look sorta sideways at folks in general. Right?"

"Won't argue the point," Slade smiled. "But it is hardly a satisfactory state of affairs. Right now we are badly in need of something definite.

"Thanks for what you told us, Bob," he said to the bartender, who had lingered after the others of the curious, the deputy, and the specials departed. "It might turn out to be a help."

"Hope so," replied Bob. "If I hear anything else I figure to be worth while I'll let you know pronto. So long; gotta go to work."

Serby stood up, cast a complacent look at the

four bodies stretched out on the floor, and said, "Guess we'd better stable our nags and amble over to Roony's for a surrounding. I'm beginning to feel mighty lank."

"I'll take a chance on a sandwich and some coffee," Slade conceded. "That's all I can risk after my snack with the farmers. First, though, I wish to mention something important: those four devils on the floor were never cowboys. Their hands conclusively prove that. Not a trace of a rope or branding-iron calluses."

"Then what were they?" demanded the bewildered sheriff.

"In my opinion, river pirates," Slade replied. "Plenty of them down around Laredo and Brownsville, but seldom do any ever get this far up the Rio Grande. So it is self-evident they were brought in by somebody familiar with the lower river, who has contacts there. Some of them can ride and shoot, as in this case. I expect that if we manage to down a few more of the bunch, we'll find that some of them, at least, are also river raiders."

"But why were they brought here?" Serby asked.

"Here's a little guesswork on my part," Slade said, "that the head of the bunch operating here worked with them elsewhere. He may have had troubles recruiting enough cowhands for the chore up here. Also, they are, as a rule, more intelligent and experienced than the average cowhand."

"Which means more trouble for us," the sheriff growled. "Oh, well, they look real purty where they are, and here's hoping we can provide 'em with a mite of company. Well, how about Roony's and that snack? I'm feeling the need of it more by the minute."

"Okay, let's go," Slade agreed.

Ten

AFTER a final pleased glance at the blanketed bodies, Serby locked the door and they cared for their horses and then headed for Roony's, where the sheriff laid a foundation with a couple of snorts and addressed himself to the repast the cook set forth. Slade sipped his coffee and munched his sandwich, slowly and with appreciation. He noted that Chet Wilfred, the Arcadia Saloon owner, was at the far end of the bar, conversing with Roony. Serby also noted his presence.

"I wonder," he said, "how he'd look with black whiskers? A sorta tall and big feller, ain't he?"

"Careful," Slade admonished. "You'll be seeing outlaws back of every glass. No reason for you to be looking sideways at Wilfred."

"Oh, I reckon I'm sorta prejudiced where rumhole owners are concerned," Serby admitted. "Not that I'd think of saying to anyone else what I just did to you. Was just thinking out loud, as it were. I'll tighten the *látigo* on my jaw till I feel I've got reasons for loosening it."

"The sensible thing to do," Slade agreed.

The sheriff chuckled. "Roony's kept everybody

away till we finished eating," he observed, "But they'll be swoopin' down soon to tell you how wonderful you are. Not that they'll be so far off."

"I can do without it," Slade sighed.

"Hafta pay a price for bein' famous," Serby pointed out. "Brace yourself! Roony's opened the corral gate, and here they come!"

Slade endured the felicitations of his well-wishers as long as he could, finally escaping on the pretext of thanking the cook for his offerings. He remained in the kitchen for some little time, chatting with the help, and when he returned to the table the interests of the crowd had shifted elsewhere.

"Wilfred left while you were in the kitchen," the sheriff remarked. "Waved to me but didn't stop. Clothes were sorta dusty, like he'd been doing considerable riding."

"Well, Gordo mentioned that after he talked with Pablo yesterday evening, he mounted a horse and rode north," Slade reminded.

"Uh-huh, that's what Gordo said," Serby returned. "Wonder where he rode to?"

"Lots of places to which he could have ridden," Slade said smilingly. "And then again he may have just ridden to no place in particular. Remember, you said yourself, once a cowhand, not happy unless forking a bronk."

Serby snorted and sampled his drink. Slade bit back a grin. He knew the old peace officer had formed an opinion concerning Chet Wilfred, and changing his opinion was something of a chore. And he was forced to admit that his deductions where men were concerned were often sound.

"Here comes Doc McChesney," the sheriff announced. "Back from the Tumbling J. This way, Doc, and have a snort and feed your tapeworm."

The old doctor accepted a chair and a drink and ordered a meal. "Just a cut scalp, no indications of fracture or concussion," he replied to Slade's question anent the pistol-whipped Tumbling J cowhand. "You did all that needed to be done. I changed the pad and bandage and let it go at that. Guess his hat sort of softened the blow, otherwise it might have killed him. Wouldn't be surprised if the hellions thought he was dead."

"Expect they did," the sheriff agreed. "You can count on it, they didn't leave him alive through kindness of heart. In too much of a hurry to get the cows moving to bother with him, I reckon. When you plan to hold the inquest on those devils we got laid out in the office?"

"After I finish eating, might as well round up a jury in here and get it over with," McChesney decided. "No sense in having the office cluttered up with the blasted vingaroons."

"Look real pretty the way they are now, but guess we'd better make room for the next batch," Serby agreed.

101

"Which, with Slade here, will be soon," Doc said. "Yep, business is going to pick up. Well, here comes my chuck, and I'm beginning to feel the need of it."

Doc took his time at dinner, then smoked a pipe before rounding up his coroner's jury. While he was at the bar, selecting some gents who could use a spare peso or so, Herman Gaunt, the Rafter H owner, entered. Glancing around, he waved to the sheriff and made his way to the bar.

"Looks like he's been doing some riding, too," remarked Serby. "All covered with dust. Well, it's getting pretty close to beef roundup time, and those fellers are sorta busy."

Slade thought the Rafter H owner also looked to be in a bad temper about something, for he glowered at his glass, his brows drawing together. He acknowledged Roony's greeting in an absent-minded manner and appeared to be studying his own reflection in the back bar mirror. Apparently he arrived at some sort of a conclusion, for he shrugged his broad shoulders, drained his glass and called for a refill, which he sipped.

Doc McChesney returned to the table, his jury trailing after him.

"Okay, Trevis, all set to go?" he said.

"Be right with you," the sheriff answered. "Ready to mosey, Walt?"

Slade was and they set out, reaching the office without incident, where the inquest quickly got under way. Slade, Serby, and Deputy Hall testified. Gordo was not called, Slade wishing to keep him as much under cover as possible.

The jury's verdict was that the four wideloopers met their death resisting arrest, with a typical cow-country rider attached that maintained it was better that way, saving the expense of the trial. Slade was singled out for special commendation. Court adjourned. The undertaker took charge of the bodies, which would go to swell the population of El Paso's already flourishing boot hill. The deputies were told to call it a night. Gordo was dispatched to Pablo Menendez' El Paso *cantina* with the word that Slade would be along shortly. Serby locked the door and he and Slade relaxed with coffee and cigarettes for a brief period.

"All this darn nonsense is more wearin' than running down owlhoots. Now what?"

"Now," Slade replied, "it's up to us to do some hard thinking and try and figure just where the devils will strike next. If we can manage to anticipate their move, there's always the chance of wiping out the whole bunch."

"You anticipated the widelooping okay," Serby reminded.

"Yes, but that one was easy, so obvious," Slade said.

"So *obvious* nobody else ever thought of it," the sheriff commented dryly.

"Past performance," Slade smiled. "Now we must look to the future."

"And you figure the hellions will hit somewhere soon, even after what happened to them last night?"

"I am positive of it," Slade answered. "*Because* of what happened to them last night. They missed out on a good haul and suffered heavy casualties. Now the head of the bunch must do something to restore morale and provide his devils with the spending money they have become accustomed to. Yes, they'll make a try for something without delay. Up to us to try and be a jump ahead of them."

"We'll jump," the sheriff predicted cheerfully. "No doubt in my mind as to that; you're not in the habit of jumping short."

"Hope your confidence will be justified," Slade replied.

"Speaking of past performance, that's what justifies my confidence," Serby retorted. "Your past performances don't leave much room for doubt where the future is concerned. How about some more coffee?"

"One more cup and we'll head for Pablo's *cantina*," Slade said. "Have a feeling he might have something to tell us."

"Here we go again!" was the blithe rejoinder as the sheriff hastened to refill the cups.

"Might as well make things cosy," he added

when he returned from the back room. Saying which, he drew the window blind and blew out the two bracket lamps, leaving only the one on the table still burning.

"Here's to more and better carcasses," he said, raising his cup.

They sipped the steaming beverage mostly in silence, each busy with his own thoughts.

Eleven

WITHOUT AN INSTANT'S WARNING, *El Halcón* shot his long arm out, sent the extinguished lamp crashing to the floor, overturned the sheriff's chair, sheriff and all, and hit the floor himself in the same flashing ripple of movement a split-second before a gun blazed in the dark back room and a slug thudded through the back of the chair he had just left. A second slug ripped across the tabletop.

Flattened on the floor, Slade drew and shot with both hands, again and yet again, spraying the back room door with lead.

A gasping cry sounded, a gurgling moan, and the sound of something falling.

"Quiet!" snapped Slade to the raving sheriff. The order was instantly obeyed, and he lay straining his ears for further sound from the back room.

The silence remained unbroken. Cautiously Slade drew a match from his pocket, flipped it alight with his thumbnail, and extinguished it even as it flamed.

But the brief flicker was enough to tell him there was nothing more to fear from the would-be drygulcher sprawled on the floor.

"Okay, now you can cuss some more," he told Serby as he struck another match and touched it to the wick of one of the bracket lamps.

The sheriff took full advantage of the permission, really outdoing himself, Slade thought.

"How in blazes did you catch on?" he concluded.

"Heard the click as he unlocked the door, then the tiny creak of the stealthily opening door—glad you didn't have the hinges well oiled—and reacted accordingly," Slade explained.

"Those ears of yours," snorted Serby. "Well, thank heaven for them. Otherwise I figure right now we'd both be cashed in."

"Not beyond the realm of possibility," Slade conceded, replacing the spent shells in his Colts with fresh cartridges. "Pretty good shooting on the devil's part, only we didn't happen to be where he thought we were and aimed."

"That door!" growled Serby. "It's always locked, and nobody ever uses it. How in blazes?"

"Most any key will manipulate the bolt of those old locks," Slade replied. "Besides, that door opens onto an alley that is nearly all the time deserted. Would have been simple to get a wax impression from which a duplicate could be made. I'd recommend that tomorrow you have brackets and a bar set in place, just in case somebody else might take a notion to enter that way. Well, let's give the gent a once-over."

The dead outlaw was turned over to reveal a rather scrubby-looking countenance that nevertheless, Slade considered, rated above the average intelligence. He examined the hands.

"Was a cowhand once, but hasn't worked at it recently," was his conclusion.

"The next work he'll do will be with a coal shovel, if what we're told about the hereafter is straight," grunted Serby.

The fellow's pockets revealed quite a bit of money, but nothing else Slade considered important.

"Not so much *dinero* as the others turned out," remarked Serby. "Expect losing that herd of cows hurt. But man! Are they after you hot and heavy!"

"But so far not having much luck catching me," Slade returned cheerfully.

Outside, excited voices were sounding. Although muffled by the walls, the shooting had evidently been heard. Somebody tried the locked door, hammered on the panels.

"Shall I let 'em in?" Serby asked.

"Sure," Slade replied. "Let them see things as they are before the body is moved."

Serby crossed the room, kicking aside the fragments of the smashed lamp and his own broken chair, and unlocked the door and flung it open.

"All right, come along and have a look," he told the gathering crowd. They filed in, exclaiming, questioning, staring at *El Halcón* and shaking their heads as Serby detailed the incident.

"Trying to gun Mr. Slade is just a nice fast way to take the Big Jump," one oldtimer expressed the consensus of opinion. "Keep up the good work, Mr. Slade, and maybe we'll have some peace and quiet hereabouts for a change."

"Don't bet on it," snorted the sheriff. "Soon as he cleans out one nest of varmints another one pops up. But it helps. Okay, some of you, now you've had a good look, pack the carcass in here and shove it against the wall. Will look better over there; floor 'pears sorta empty and lonesome with no sidewinders on it. Anyhow, I've got to scrub the blood off the back room floor."

However, eager volunteers took over that chore.

Serby let the crowd, constantly augmented by new arrivals, loiter for a while, then shooed everybody out and locked the door again.

"Now what?" he asked the ranger.

"Guess we might as well make our try for Pablo's *cantina*," Slade decided. "We won't have any peace here. The word will be getting around and more gents will be headed this way pronto."

"You're darn right," said Serby. "Let's go!" He blew out the bracket lamp and they left the office and barely missed being intercepted by a bunch rounding a far corner.

Without further misadventure, they reached the

cantina, where they found Carmen, Pablo, and Gordo anxiously awaiting them.

"We heard there was shooting up around the courthouse, and of course we figured at once that you two were mixed up in it some way. Tell us about it," said Carmen.

Serby at once launched into a vivid account of the happenings in the office.

"The hellions got no respect for anything," he concluded. "Shootin' up the sheriff's office! And if it wasn't for Walt's ears, and gun hands, the chances are they'd have gotten away with it. I'm beginning to think it's the worst bunch we ever went up against. Even Walt don't 'pear to have any notion as to who they are and who's the head of the pack."

"Be not so sure," Pablo rejoined shrewdly. "*Capitán* does not always speak of what he thinks, or knows.

"The *Señor* Gaunt was here earlier in the evening," he added. "He asked, *Capitán*, were you around. Intimated he wished to congratulate you on saving the *Señor* Judson's cattle. Said he felt the less fear now for his own stock. Him I told that there would be in the *Señor* Sheriff's office an inquest, later, and that doubtless he could you find there."

Slade nodded, his eyes thoughtful, but did not comment.

"Guess I'm in the market for a surrounding,

110

Pablo," Serby said. "Had my dinner at Roony's, but that was quite a while ago and a lot has happened in between."

"I know how you feel," said Carmen. "I was too bothered to eat, and now I'm starved. How about you, Walt?"

"Well, seeing as a single sandwich is all I've partaken of since early afternoon, I'm inclined to join you," Slade replied.

"Too will I," said Pablo. "And Gordo is hungry always, so the party we will have. Waiter!"

It was a very pleasant party, and by the time it was over, the hour was late, so everybody called it a night.

The middle of the following afternoon found Slade and the sheriff in the office awaiting the arrival of Doctor McChesney and his jury to hold his inquest over the latest gent to indulge in the folly of trading shots with *El Halcón*.

"Didn't I say business was going to pick up?" chuckled old Doc as he rolled in.

"And it's liable to really pick up tomorrow," said Serby. "Tomorrow is payday for the rail-roads, and for most of the spreads, too. Yep, things will boom tomorrow night. Looked for a while that the paycar might not make it today; bad freight wreck down to the east of Clint, but they figure to get the mess cleaned up by dark. Paycar will be a mite late reaching town this evening but not enough to greatly matter. Paymaster will have his envelopes filled in time to shove 'em out tomorrow morning."

"Will be quite a passel of money in that car," Doc observed. "With the roads clumping together and using the same car for reasons of economy and not cluttering up the yard more than necessary. Of course, the railroad police will be guarding it. Well, here come my loafers, so we'll get this chore over with."

It didn't take long. Slade and the sheriff were exonerated of blame and congratulated. The body was carted away. The coroner and the jury departed in quest of refreshment. Slade and the sheriff settled down to talk things over.

"Well, what do you think?" Serby asked.

"I think," Slade replied soberly, "that you and I had better be on our toes tonight."

"You mean you believe the hellions might make a try for that car?" the sheriff said incredulously.

"It really doesn't seem reasonable that they should," Slade conceded. "But something that appears, on the surface, to be utterly unreasonable may well pose a challenge to such a genius as is without doubt operating in the section. Look for the unexpected and you're liable not to be wrong. If they do make a try, it will be in a novel and unlooked-for manner calculated to catch everybody flat-footed. Our chore is not to be of the 'everybody.' "

"That's a hard one to unscramble, but I calc'late to get what you mean, sorta at least," growled the sheriff. "In good plain Texas talk, we've got to get the jump on the devils 'fore they get the jump on us."

"That's the general idea," Slade smiled. "Well, it's a nice day, so I think I'll amble around town a bit."

"And from all indications, tomorrow will be another nice one, and a nice day on payday, with everybody rolling in, means it won't be anything nice for me," grumbled Serby. "I'm swearing in a few specials I can trust to lend a hand if needed. Okay, meet you at Roony's for dinner. Right?"

"Okay," Slade agreed. "At just about dark."

"And you watch your step," the sheriff cautioned. "They're sure after you, and I don't mean maybe."

"I'll do my best," Slade promised carelessly. Serby let go a disgusted snort as he passed out, closing the door behind him.

It was a beautiful day and Slade enjoyed his stroll. Everywhere was an air of expectancy, for payday was always an event at a border town. And that was just what El Paso still was despite its claim to being a city—a wild border town— and would be for quite some time to come.

Studying faces, listening to scraps of conversation, Slade walked the streets, dropping into several places where he was known, including

McGinty's, where he chatted with Bob, the bartender.

"Nope, ain't seen the big jigger with the whiskers I told you about as being with those blankety-blank wideloopers you did in," Bob replied to a question. "If I do, I'll give him a careful once-over and get in touch with you."

Slade thanked him and continued his saunter. He reached the waterfront and for some time stood watching the bustling activities. Workers who remembered him from former visits shouted greetings. A foreman paused for a gab.

Leaving the wharf, he obeyed a sudden impulse and turned his steps to the nearby Arcadia Saloon, which had been robbed, a bartender murdered. He had visited the place on a former occasion, but not since it changed ownership.

The moment he stepped through the swinging doors, he noted a marked improvement. The place had been rather slovenly and run in a somewhat slipshod manner. Now the furnishings were new and in good taste. The long bar shone like a mirror; the lunch counter appeared spotlessly clean. There were two roulette wheels, a faro bank, tables for games, others for leisurely dining. A partition had been knocked out to enlarge the dance floor. The girls were just coming on and were young, pretty, and looked nice. The two bartenders wore white coats and black ties and gave a spruce appearance. The same went for the waiters.

The new owner, tall, rugged-featured Chet Wilfred, was at the far end of the bar. He spotted *El Halcón* at once and hurried to greet him.

"How are you, Mr. Slade?" he said. "Glad to have you with us. Sit down and have a couple on the house."

Slade accepted, for he welcomed the opportunity to study Chet Wilfred at close range. A waiter came to take his order. They raised glasses in mutual salute.

"Been in the liquor business before?" Slade asked casually.

Wilfred looked contemplative. "Yes, in a way," he replied. "I'll tell you about it, if you don't mind listening."

"Be glad to," Slade answered.

"As I expect you've already guessed, I was born and brought up on a ranch," Wilfred began. "Over in the Sabine River country. A not very large spread, but a good one. When my dad died, I inherited the holding. But about that time, some years back, the cattle business was sort of in the doldrums, and when I got a chance to sell at what I considered a good price, I took advantage of the opportunity. Was at loose ends, as it were. Banked the money, not too large an amount, and worked at quite a few things. Was always handy with cards and dealt some on the river boats,

115

which, as you no doubt know, paid pretty well. Made out fairly well at poker on the side, and banked my winnings. In the course of my work on the boats, I became acquainted with a gent who owned a saloon in Houston. The upshot of that, I went to work for him. Stayed with him a couple of years and learned about all there was to learn about the saloon business. Saw there was money in it if handled right. Could have opened a small place in Houston, but I'd grown weary of the big town. Packed up my traps and headed west. In fact, I had Arizona or California in mind, but I stopped off here at El Paso, liked the town, liked the section, and when I learned old Sam Mumford was anxious to sell out, I jumped at the chance. Fixed the place up a bit and am doing pretty well. Still got a certain amount of hair rope and horse flesh in my blood, I guess. Anyhow, I do quite a bit of riding around and looking things over." He chuckled, a gleam of amusement in his eyes, which Slade now saw were very light blue.

"All of which rigmarole, explaining my riding around and so forth, brings me to something I feel might interest you."

"Yes?" Slade prompted.

"The other night, when it was so cloudy and windy, with rain now and then, I was riding back from Clint. I'd gotten to not so very far east of where the lightning smashed a hole in the river bank and changed its course when the clouds thinned a little, letting some moonlight through. I happened to look and saw, just topping a rise a couple of hundred yards behind, seven riders coming toward me pretty fast. I felt the chances were they were just some cowpokes heading home, but it's a mighty lonely trail along there and I figured to play it safe. So I shoved my bronk into the edge of the brush where I was sure I wouldn't be spotted and waited for those gents to pass."

Wilfred paused to sip his drink and twinkled his eyes at Slade, who sat expectant.

"I'd already noticed that they had their hatbrims pulled real low, their neckerchiefs real high, as if they preferred nobody get a good look at them, which struck me sorta funny. As it happened, I did get a pretty good look at them. Maybe ten or twelve yards from where I sat my cayuse, they reined in and looked down toward the river, talking together—couldn't make out what they said. They 'peared to be a sorta average bunch except one, a tall and broad jigger with a heavy black beard.

"And now I'm coming to what I really think will interest you," he continued. "The big fellow sure had a familiar look—his build, the way he carried himself. I could swear I'd seen him somewhere, though just where and when I hadn't the slightest notion, still don't have.

"Well, they talked together for a minute, then turned from the trail and rode north across the prairie; I watched them out of sight—clouds were thickening again—and continued on my way to town. Figured the chances were I was just being silly and 'seeing' things, and forgot all about it. But when the next day I heard about your run-in with the seven wideloopers, it came back to me, and I was pretty well convinced that the seven riders I saw *were* the wideloopers, the big fellow the leader of the pack and one of those that slid out of the loop. What do you think?"

"Sounds like a logical deduction," Slade replied. "Do you think you'd recognize the big fellow if you happened to see him again, especially without a beard?"

Wilfred hesitated a moment before answering. "Frankly, I fear I could not, to the extent of being able to definitely say, 'That is the man.' I didn't get a good look at his face; it was his build and carriage that seemed to strike a chord of memory. If I were to see him under similar circumstances and conditions, say sitting a horse in misty moonlight, it might be otherwise. The whole matter is rather baffling, but I felt you should know about it, on the chance it might prove of value."

"It could," Slade said. "And thank you for telling me. Well, I'll have to be going; am eating dinner with the sheriff and it's about that time."

"And please drop in again soon," Wilfred begged.

"I will," Slade promised, and meant it.

Twelve

AS HE HEADED FOR ROONY'S, Slade rehashed the conversation, which had been very much in the nature of a monologue. He felt it would require some thought to properly evaluate it. Upon reaching the saloon, he put it aside for the time being, for keeping Serby company at their table was old Sime Judson, the Tumbling J owner.

"Went down and made up with the Mexican farmers," Judson announced, after shaking hands warmly. "Had me quite a time. It's a *fiesta* today, and they had knocked off work and were doing a mite of celebrating. Lots of wine, good chuck, music, and dancing, and everybody having a good time. These fellers are all right, once you get to really know them, as I've already started telling the boys."

Which Slade thought made very pleasant hearing. The danger of real border trouble was fast diminishing. Something worth while accomplished.

"I'm full to the ears." Judson declined an invitation to join them at dinner. "When those fellers down by the river feed you, you're fed. I see a couple of the boys from the northeast spreads at the bar; think I'll go over and have a gab with them."

Slade and the sheriff enjoyed a leisurely dinner, mostly in silence, as good food deserved. Not until they had finished eating and pipe and cigarette were going strong did Slade repeat his conversation with Chet Wilfred for the sheriff's edification.

Serby listened intently, muttering under his mustache from time to time.

"So it looks like Wilfred, a jigger I been sorta keeping an eye on, is out as a suspect," he commented when the ranger paused.

"Not necessarily," Slade differed. "Wilfred is undoubtedly an able man, highly intelligent and educated. He could very well have concocted that yarn to draw attention from himself.

"Not that I'm intimating any such thing; so far I have no reason to do so, but it is a possibility that must be given consideration. Until and unless we unearth something that definitely points to off-color practices on his part, we must hold our judgment in abeyance where Chet Wilfred is concerned. As I've said, so long as we have no conclusive suspect, everybody is suspect. Did the paycar make it to town?"

"A little before you came in," Serby replied. "Settin' on that spur right across from the street that parallels the yards on the south, where they usually spot it, just a little ways from the street. A couple of the railroad police standing guard over it, with maybe another one or two hid somewhere in the dark, although I doubt it. Never knew 'em to post more than two."

"I'm familiar with that street," Slade said thoughtfully. "A single line of buildings on the south side, warehouses and supply depots, closed at night, and dark. Street is at a slightly higher level than the yards. The spur which accommodates the paycar is only about fifty or sixty feet from the street. Just to the north of the spur is a main lead from a gravity hump."

"Yep, that's it," nodded Serby. "Won't be a great deal of work in the yards after midnight tonight, giving the boys a chance to get ready for their payday bust. Be plenty busy for the next three or four hours, though. And you think there's a chance the devils will make a try for the money in that car?"

"It doesn't seem reasonable, that guarded car in the busy yard, but somehow I've a hunch they will."

"And your hunches are about one hundred percent straight, I've noticed," the sheriff said. "How or why, I'm darned if I know, but they are."

"Well, my great-grandmother on my mother's side was born and brought up in the Scottish glens and firmly believed in the second sight whereby a person can foresee future events," Slade replied smilingly. "Perhaps something of it filtered down to me, for many declare it is hereditary."

"More likely figuring all the angles correctly and then tying 'em up right," the sheriff observed shrewdly. "If they do make a try, will it be after midnight when things are quiet?"

Slade shook his head. "By then the paymaster would have his envelopes filled and the money stashed in the safe," he explained. "It's a new steel safe and couldn't be opened quickly. If it is made at all, the attempt will be made while the safe is still open, most of the money and the filled envelopes on the table in front of the paymaster. How? I haven't the slightest notion, although I do believe that if a try is made, it will be an hour or so before midnight, when everybody is rushing around getting their last chores done."

"Sounds like that makes sense," Serby agreed. "Now what?"

"Now I think it would be a good idea to mosey down to Pablo's *cantina* for a while," Slade decided.

"I believe handling it this way may tend to lull the suspicions of anybody who may be keeping tabs on us," he continued as they set out. "I think it unlikely that anybody is, but with such a bunch as we are up against, it's best not to take chances."

"Sure for certain," growled the sheriff. "After shooting up my office as they did, I figure there ain't anything past them. Liable to pull a rabbit outa the hat at any time. Quiet tonight, ain't it? But that's usually the way the night before payday, folks building up their strength for the bust."

When they reached the *cantina*, they found it also unusually quiet, with much less than the normal night crowd present.

"Nice and peaceful for a change," Carmen remarked as she joined them at their favorite table. "Some of our regulars dropped in but didn't stay long. Said they needed to rest up for tomorrow night. Mr. Preston Owen of the Circle B was here for a little while. Asked about you, Walt— he always does—and Mr. Gaunt, who stopped for a few minutes, also asked if you'd been around. I told him I expected you later."

Slade nodded, but did not comment. Carmen had a glass of wine with them and then departed for the back room.

"Got quite a bit of paper work to catch up with," she explained. "And I must check stock against tomorrow. Try and keep out of trouble till I join you; will be quite a while, however." She flashed him a smile as she trotted away. Slade gazed at the clock.

"Another half-hour and we'll move," he announced.

"Okay," answered Serby. "Here comes Gordo Allendes."

"Good!" Slade exclaimed. "We'll take him with us. May need another man, but I figured it wasn't wise to contact the deputies or the specials; might attract attention, with somebody guessing correctly why we were rounding them up."

"Right," said the sheriff, beckoning the knife-man to join them. "Gordo'll be rarin' to go."

Gordo was "rarin' to go." His black eyes sparkled and his teeth flashed in a delighted grin.

"My blade, it thirsts," he said.

Shortly, he finished his glass of wine and glanced suggestively at Slade, who in turn glanced at the clock, and swept the room with his eyes.

Carmen was in the back room with the door closed, Pablo busy at the far end of the bar. Slade nodded to his companions, and they eased through the swinging doors.

"Straight to the street south of the one that faces the yards," *El Halcón* said.

He continually scanned the back track as they walked, but saw nothing that looked like somebody following them. Reaching the street in question, he turned down it and led the way for some distance before he halted where there was a narrow crack between two buildings.

For minutes he stood motionless surveying

the way they had come. Finally he said, "Looks okay so far. Into the alley and take it easy. We should have a good view of the yards from where it opens onto the next street."

The "alley" was barely wide enough for them to get their shoulders through, and very dark, but there were no obstructions and without difficulty they reached the point where it opened onto the next street. Here it was a trifle wider and, clumped together, they studied the busy yards, at once spotting the paycar, which was lighted. Slade could just make out the shadowy forms of the two railroad policemen standing guard, one on either side of the rear platform. He thought it very likely that there were another or two somewhere in the darkness. He estimated the distance to the car.

"Better than fifty yards," he murmured to the others. "Wish we could get a bit closer, but here is the only spot where we can be holed up and out of sight. Have to make the best of it if something does cut loose."

He studied the yard, which was plenty busy. Standing on a lead just north of the paycar and near the foot of a gravity hump, a big locomotive, apparently unoccupied at the moment, purred under a full head of steam. Slade's glance passed over it and centered on the paycar. Everything appeared peaceful there, with no indications of alarm.

"Getting close to midnight," he muttered. "If something is going to happen, it'll be soon. For the life of me I can't figure what or how."

It happened!

Thirteen

SUDDENLY the locomotive stack boomed, belching a cloud of smoke and clots of fire. Slade was sure he saw a shadowy form dart away into the darkness as the drivers spun, caught, and the big engine went rocketing down the lead, gaining speed with every turn of the wheels, straight for where a red light marked an open switch to a track on which stood a string of loaded cars.

For a moment the posse stood paralyzed with astonishment at this utterly unexpected development.

The runaway engine screeched through the switch and hit the string of cars with a deafening crash. The boiler exploded with a roar. Flaming coals were scattered far and wide.

And knifing through the bellow of escaping steam, Slade's keen ears caught a crackle of gunfire.

"Come on!" he shouted. "This is it! To the car! To the car!"

With *El Halcón* well in the lead, the posse dashed from concealment and down the slope to the tracks.

The yard was pandemonium plus ultra, apparently everybody bawling, cursing, questioning, running toward the steaming fragments of the locomotive. A gondola car loaded with creosoted crossties had been overturned and its highly inflammable contents were burning merrily. The paycar was utterly forgotten.

That is, except by *El Halcón* and his two companions, who were converging on it, guns ready for business.

The distance to cover was less than sixty yards, but to Walt Slade, beset by a dreadful anxiety for the paymaster and others, it stretched to whole furlongs, the seconds to reach the car a handspan of eternity.

One of the yard police lay near the platform steps, unconscious and bleeding from a head wound, his gun beside him. The other was nowhere in sight. Slade bounded up the steps to the platform, Gordo crowding almost beside him, the sheriff close behind, and through the open door.

The paymaster, white, shaking, was crouched in a corner, a masked man holding a gun on him. There were six more masked men in the compartment, one busily stuffing money-filled envelopes into a canvas sack; the others, guns in hand. On the table, a single shaded lamp burned. Standing beside it, a tall, broad-shouldered individual who appeared to be superintending matters. All whirled toward the door as the posse bulged in.

"Down!" Slade shouted, hurling himself to the floor, shooting with both hands.

The tall man smashed the lamp with a sweep of his gun barrel. Darkness swooped down like a thrown blanket. The car literally exploded to the bellow of sixshooters.

Over went the table with a crash. A boomed order, boots beat the floor! The bang and rattle of flung-open doors, more running steps.

"After them, through the back!" Slade roared. He leaped to his feet, dashed for the back door of the compartment, and fell over the smashed table, striking the floor with stunning force. As he tried to scramble erect, Gordo fell over *him*. The cursing sheriff lurched into the tangle, which didn't help matters. The back door of the car banged open and boots thudded on the ground, going away from there fast.

"Hold it!" Slade called to his companions. "They made it in the clear and there's no catching them up in the dark. Try and light one of those bracket lamps, Trevis." He made it to his feet as he spoke and this time managed to stay on them.

A light flashed up. The paymaster, familiar with the layout, had struck a match to a lamp directly over where he had crouched.

"That's fine," Slade told him. "Well, looks like the night is not a total loss."

There were three dead men sprawled on the floor, one still gripping the sack full of money envelopes.

"They didn't have time to clean the safe?" Slade asked the paymaster, a dignified, elderly individual, who had recovered from his fright.

"That's right," the other replied. "They were just starting to when you gentlemen showed up. Sheriff Serby, is it not?"

"That's so," the sheriff admitted. "And this is Mr. Slade, my special deputy. You can thank him for saving your payroll money, and maybe yourself; it's a killer bunch." The paymaster shivered and shot Slade a grateful look.

"And this is Gordo, who took care of one of those devils on the floor," Slade said, gesturing to the haft of the long knife that skewered a dead outlaw's throat.

"Now I want a look at that wounded yard policeman," he added.

Outside was the sound of approaching feet, and cries and exclamations. Slade stepped to the door and his great voice stilled the tumult.

"Bring a lantern, one of you fellows," he ordered. "That's right, hold it close."

With his sensitive fingers he probed the vicinity of the wound, nodded with relief.

"Not too bad, just creased," he announced. "Send somebody to fetch Doc McChesney."

"I'll take care of it, Walt," said a voice of

authority. The newcomer was Ed Colter, the night yardmaster, whom Slade knew well.

"Here's the other police feller, over here by the end of the car," somebody called. "Got his head cut open, too."

Slade performed another examination. "Got a nasty lick, with a gun barrel, the chances are, but I can't ascertain any indications of fracture," was his diagnosis. "Doc will look after him. Here comes the fire company," he added as clanging bells drew near. "Guess the yard boys have gotten the blaze pretty well under control already."

The paymaster stuck his head out the car door. "Will somebody help me clear up this mess in here so I can get the rest of the envelopes filled for you to have tomorrow?"

Without delay, there were plenty of volunteers to take care of that chore.

"And, Ed, we'd take it kind if you'd have some of your boys pack the carcasses to my office," Serby said to the yardmaster.

"Coming right up," replied Colter, rattling off a number of names.

"How that infernal engine managed to kick open the throttle and get going down the lead is beyond me," he growled. "Evidently the brakes weren't set, either. Somebody is going to hear about that."

"Never mind scolding your boys for something

which they were not responsible for," Slade told him. "That engine getting loose was not an accident as a result of somebody's carelessness. It was an example of hairtrigger thinking and the instant grasp of an opportunity that would provide the diversion needed to consummate the robbery. I got a glimpse of the hellion running away from it after he opened the throttle and released the brakes. Hope he is one of those the boys are packing to the sheriff's office. Expect, though, he went to keep an eye on their horses, and hightailed when he saw the jig was up."

"Do you ever miss anything!" groaned the yardmaster. "I never thought of that angle. But of course *you* did. Here comes Doc. Maybe those two police will have something to tell us when they get their senses back."

"Possibly," Slade said. "One did manage to get his gun going, I believe."

The doctor turned to Slade. "You say there's no indication of fracture? Well, if you say there ain't, there ain't. I'll patch 'em up, give them a stimulant, and have them carried to my office for the night. You can question them tomorrow, if you wish. Won't hold an inquest tomorrow, seeing as it's payday."

"A notion," agreed Serby.

Before the bodies were moved, the masks were stripped off, revealing hard-lined countenances with nothing outstanding about them, so far as

132

Slade could see. Nobody present recalled seeing them before.

"We'll look them over more closely at the office," Slade said. "Gordo, trot down to the *cantina* and tell Carmen and Pablo that we're all right and will be seeing them shortly."

"Maybe they're in the crowd up there on the street," chuckled the sheriff. " 'Pears everybody in town is here."

"What with the crash, the explosion, and all the shooting, it's not remarkable," Slade replied. "Everything considered we came out of it quite well, even though the head hellion made good his escape again. Neither of us got so much as a scratch."

"Yep, your trick of hitting the floor as the lamp went out served us mighty well; the devils shot over us," nodded Serby.

"They were caught completely off balance," Slade said. "I imagine we were the last persons in the world they expected to be present. They must have thought their plan was working with the precision of a well-oiled machine."

"Would have were it not for *El Halcón* tossing a monkey wrench into the machine," Serby observed cheerfully. "Well, guess we might as well mosey to the office for a few minutes, then to Pablo's and call it a night. Okay?"

"A good idea," Slade agreed. "Let's go."

There were others besides the railroaders

in the office when they arrived there. Several persons were sure they had seen one or more of the unsavory trio in town, but recalled little concerning them. Finally the sheriff shooed out Slade's admirers who were profuse in their praise, and the contents of the outlaws' pockets were examined.

"Each bunch shows a bit less money than the ones before," Serby commented. "I've a notion the horned toads are getting a mite short on spendin' cash."

"Which bodes no good for us," Slade said. "We can look for trouble, soon. A morale boost and a good haul are essential to the head of the outfit if he hopes to keep his followers in line.

"Also," he added soberly, "he will need more money to consummate the really big project he has in mind."

"How's that?" the sheriff asked, looking puzzled.

"We'll discuss it later," Slade replied. "I'm not quite ready to talk about it. Have a move on my own to make first. If that works out as I hope, and really expect, it will go a long ways toward clearing up the mystery as to who is head of the bunch, for it will provide the motivation back of his presence and activities here."

Serby heaved a sigh, "Here we go again! Oh, well, I knew it was but a matter of time till you figured where to twirl your loop."

"But still have to figure how to make the cast," Slade smiled.

"Just a matter of time, just a matter of time," Serby repeated. "Well, I don't see anything of any account in this junk from their pockets, 'sides from the *dinero*."

"But once again, there's something of account, their hands, that show conclusively they were never range riders, though they dress the part," Slade said.

"More river pirates, eh?"

"Looks that way," Slade replied. "Well, with former contacts with the brand handled in a satisfactory manner, we won't bother our heads too much about them."

"Right," said the sheriff. "All set to head for the *cantina*?"

Slade intimated he was, so with a last glance at the blanketed forms on the floor, they locked the door and set out, walking the almost deserted streets.

Without misadventure they reached the *cantina*, where they found Carmen had already changed to a street dress and Pablo was ready to sound his last call.

"I was plenty jittery until Gordo showed up," the girl admitted. "Couldn't imagine what in the world had happened but knew very well you were mixed up in it somehow. Well, tomorrow's the big day, and we'd better make ready for it." She glanced through her lashes at Slade.

"One snort," put in the sheriff, "and we'll call it a night."

To which everybody agreed.

Fourteen

PRETTY WELL WORN OUT by the hectic night, Slade slept until well past noon. After shaving and cleaning up generally, he set out for the sheriff's office through the golden sunshine of a beautiful day. He found that peace officer puffing his pipe and contemplating the bodies on the floor.

"Enjoying the scenery," he explained. "They look real pretty like that. Sorta lonesome, though. Guess we'll have to rustle some company for them. Shouldn't be hard to do today, or, more specially, tonight. If we get past this one without some hell bustin' loose, I'll be surprised; the *loco* coots are already whooping it up. Thanks to you, the paymaster is handing out the envelopes. And the hands from the nearer spreads are riding in. Yep, I got a feeling this one is going to be a lulu."

"And may provide opportunity for our owlhoot *amigos*," Slade pointed out. "Which in turn might provide opportunity for us, if we can just play the hand right."

"Wait till I pour some coffee and we'll try to do a mite of figuring," said Serby. "And you believe the devils might take advantage of the payday bust to pull something, eh?"

"I certainly do," the ranger replied. "It's up to us to figure what and where."

The coffee was soon forthcoming, Serby spiking his liberally from a bottle in the desk drawer. The two law-enforcement officers went into executive session, with no satisfactory conclusions. That a master mind, planning and directing operations, existed there was little doubt. Who? Slade was beginning to get a notion with not much on which to base it. Depending largely on the process of elimination which narrowed down possible suspects.

Find the motive, says the "book" of the rangers—not a book of printed pages—and you are well on the way to corraling your man. Slade was positive he had found the motive, his deductions foundationed on his unusual technical knowledge of natural phenomena. Who would profit from the motive? First, someone who also possessed the needed technical knowledge. Second, someone who had or hoped to amass the money necessary to the consummation of the project. Abruptly, Slade pushed back his empty cup and stood up.

"Going to take a little stroll," he announced. "Won't be gone long. After which we'll drop in at Roony's and see how things are going there."

"Okay," nodded Serby. "I'll be here waiting

for you. Watch your step." He did not suggest accompanying the ranger, knowing that he had something in mind that he preferred to handle alone.

Leaving the office, Slade did not stroll aimlessly but walked straight to the railroad telegraph office where the operator on duty, an old acquaintance, greeted him warmly.

"Something I can do for you, Mr. Slade?" he asked.

"Wish to send a wire, Tommy, confidential," *El Halcón* replied.

"Certain," said the operator. "Let's have it."

Writing out a carefully worded message addressed to a Land Office official, a close friend, Slade handed it to the operator, who glanced at it, opened his key.

"Should have a reply in a couple of hours or so," *El Halcón* said. "Hold it for me, of course."

"Certain," the operator repeated. "Say! the boys are sure swearing by you today. If it wasn't for you, they'd have been late for their payday bust. A fine chore you did, a fine chore."

"I got the breaks," Slade smiled.

"Huh! Us fellers have a different word for it," the operator replied. "Be seeing you."

"Be seeing you, Tommy."

Outside the office, Slade remarked to the cigarette he was rolling, "Well, the answer to that wire may break the case wide open. Here's hoping, for I sure don't know of anything else that has a chance to."

He walked slowly back to the sheriff's office, enjoying the colorful scene, for now the payday celebration was getting well under way and would soon be in full swing. Music and song and a patter of whirling words billowed over the swinging doors. On the dance floors high heels clicked and boots thumped. The roulette wheels spun merrily, the little balls bouncing from slot to slot to the accompaniment of whoops or growls, depending on who guessed right and who didn't. Gold pieces clanged on the "mahogany," with the chink of bottle necks on glass rims providing a cheerful undertone. All was gaiety, mirth, and good fellowship, so far. Would be different later on when the redeye that was being consumed in quantities began really getting in its licks.

Now the cowhands from the more distant spreads were bulging into town, their horses' irons kicking up little spurtles of dust as they were trotted to the nearest hitchracks and their owners dived into the nearest saloons.

The weather was cooperating beautifully to make the celebration a success, warm and bright, with just enough breeze to temper the heat. Payday in a border town! Slade felt his pulses quicken, for he was honest with himself in admitting that he liked it.

So did sprightly old Sheriff Serby, for that

matter, although he growled disgustedly when Slade arrived.

"Listen to the *loco* coots beller," he snorted. "Didn't I tell you it was going to be a wild one? Well, how about Roony's and a couple of swallers and a snack?"

"Guess we should get in the spirit of things," Slade agreed. "Reckon your pets on the floor there will stay put. Anybody else recall seeing them before?"

"Oh, some barkeeps were pretty sure they'd served them at one time or another but didn't remember anything much about them, just some passin' through hellions like dozens more of the same brand all the time showing up and then disappearin'. Let's go!"

They found the big saloon and restaurant plenty lively, and growing more so by the minute. Already it was quite crowded, but Roony had reserved their favorite table and conducted them to it to the accompaniment of whooped greetings from the railroaders at the bar, and beckoned a waiter to take their orders, full dinners for both.

"Didn't take time for breakfast," observed the sheriff. "How about you?"

"Same applies," Slade admitted. "Wanted to contact you before I ate."

"Suppose Carmen went to work early today," Serby remarked casually.

"I suppose she did," Slade conceded smilingly. The sheriff chuckled.

When the food arrived, it was plain that the Mexican cook had *El Halcón* in mind and surpassed even his habitual culinary efforts.

"Yes, as I've said before, eating with you is a calamity," the sheriff declared. "That jigger could serve up an old rubber boot so it would be tasty. Pounds and pounds! At this rate, I'll soon be waddlin' like a blasted duck. Guess I'd better have another snort to sorta even things up."

Slade had another cup of coffee and a cigarette, then glanced at the clock.

"Be back shortly," he said. "You take it easy for a little while. After I return, the chances are we'll amble down to Pablo's *cantina*. Always the chance that he or Gordo will have something to tell us."

Leaving the saloon, Slade repaired to the telegraph office. The operator, without speaking, handed him a sealed envelope. Slade tore it open and read the Land Office official's reply to his message. It consisted of but two words, that spelled a name. Slade gazed at it a moment, then tore the telegram to small pieces and stuffed them in a pocket.

"Thank you, Tommy," he told the operator. "May turn out to be a big help."

"Always glad to lend a hand, Mr. Slade," the operator replied. "Be seeing you."

Now the streets were really hopping, and Slade had to squirm his way through the swirling throng that packed the sidewalks and spilled out onto the roadway where pedestrians dodged horsemen and cursed them jovially. Most anything goes on payday.

Slade walked slowly, endeavoring to evaluate what he had learned from his friend at the Land Office, which confirmed his own deductions in a satisfying manner. He had the motive, and he believed he now knew the identity of the leader of the outlaw bunch, who stood to profit hugely were he able to consummate the fantastic scheme he had evolved, concerned only with his own selfish ends, heedless of the sorrow and suffering that would be visited upon others.

And between those innocents and the monster of greed and iniquity stood only *El Halcón*. But *El Halcón*, said the lowly, walked in the shadow of God's hand.

Pausing, Slade gazed toward Cordova Island. He wondered was it from that man-made island the ruthless devil got the inspiration for his scheme.

One thing was sure for certain; he was a genius of a high order. A pity, Slade thought, that so able a man should for some unknown reason take the wrong fork in the trail. Well, it wasn't the first of that sort he had pitted guns and wits with, and doubtless would not be the last, presupposing that he, Slade, would come out top dog in this particular instance. Well, he'd take a chance on that, hoping that as the past had been, so would be the present and the future. He strolled on with a carefree mind.

When he reached Roony's, he found that rumhole—the sheriff's designation of it— bursting at the seams. The bar was lined three deep, the dance floor so crowded the couples could barely shuffle, every table occupied, roulette wheels and faro bank doing plenty of business.

"So, back in one piece, eh?" remarked the sheriff. "Was beginning to worry about you a mite; was scairt you might have got tromped down out there. Blazes, what a crowd! Never saw the like. Deputy Hall and a couple of the specials were in. Reported not bad trouble, so far. But just wait! All set to make for Pablo's?"

"A good idea, I guess," Slade replied. They waved to Roony and headed for the door.

"By the way," Serby said, "Doc McChesney had a few words with those two railroad police fellers after they got their senses back. Seems they didn't know from nothin'. The one that got whacked with a gun barrel couldn't remember anything except that all of a sudden he saw stars and comets and the lights went out. The other saw the devils coming at him and managed to draw his gun, but was creased before he could squeeze trigger. Doc gave 'em a sedative and said you could talk with them after it wears off, if you want to."

"Be just a waste of time," Slade replied. "I expected as much. Say! There is quite a crowd out tonight."

"*Loco* hellions!" growled the sheriff. "Listen to 'em whoop. Come to think of it, wasn't the big jigger who got away last night wearin' whiskers under the mask?"

"He was," Slade agreed. "I got a glimpse of them as he knocked the lamp over. A false beard is his disguise, and appears to fool everybody, which is, of course, what he desires, keeping folks looking for a bearded individual who is *not* bearded at other times."

"That is, everybody except *El Halcón*," Serby pointed out. "Well, here we are. Let's see how this rumhole is doing."

Although perhaps a little less noisy, the lighting more subdued, the *cantina* was as crowded and busy as Roony's. Shouts greeted them as they entered. Gordo Allendes was lounging at the near end of the bar.

Serby continued to the table Pablo had reserved for them, but Slade paused for a few words with Gordo. He gave the knifeman some precise and surprising instructions.

However, Gordo did not appear surprised; nothing, it seemed, ever surprised him. He bowed low as he accepted a glass of wine, and said, "Done it will be, *Capitán*." After finishing his wine, he would drift through the swinging doors to take care of the chore to which he had been assigned.

Slade joined Serby at the table. Carmen trotted over from the dance floor and plumped into a chair beside Slade, which she shifted closer. She slanted him a laughing glance through her lashes.

"So you finally made it," she said. "Perhaps you can put in one night without getting mixed up in something."

"If we do get mixed up in something, I'll be the one to be surprised," Slade told her. "Where mix-ups are concerned, my head is empty as a dried *calabaza* gourd."

"Please keep it that way," she begged. "After last night, a little peace and quiet would sure be welcome. Yes, I'll have a glass of wine and then back to the floor for a while. Business is booming tonight. Later you'll have to dance with me. And that isn't all; I'll tell you what else before long."

"Sounds interesting," interpolated the sheriff. Carmen wrinkled her nose at him.

Slade had a very good idea as to what she had in mind, but he merely smiled, and didn't differ with her. She finished her wine and scampered off to the floor.

The sheriff glanced about and shook his head disapprovingly.

"*Loco* guzzlers!" he grumbled. "Don't know from straight up!"

" 'O that men should put an enemy in their mouths to steal away their brains!' " Slade misquoted slightly with a smile.

"What brains?" snorted Serby. "Waiter!" The waiter in question hurried to refill a "guzzle" glass. The sheriff chuckled as he noted Carmen was conferring with the orchestra leader; he knew what that meant.

Slade knew also, for when Carmen beckoned, he rose to his feet and strolled to the raised platform which accommodated the musicians.

The leader stepped to the edge of the platform, waving a guitar; his voice rang out. "*Señoritas, Señores*! Attention, please, and silence! *Capitán* will sing." He bowed low, handed the guitar to *El Halcón*, and retired.

Making sure the instrument was tuned to his liking, Slade played a sprightly prelude, flashed the white smile of *El Halcón* at his expectant audience, flung back his head, and sang.

Music! The universal language that makes the whole world kin. And when translated by such a voice as Walt Slade's great, golden baritone-bass, it weaves a web of brotherhood such as no other medium can.

Of the rangeland he sang, of the hills and the valleys, the mountains and the streams. His rapt listeners could hear the low thunder of the marching herd, view the glow of the campfire, where the toil of the day was forgotten in gaiety and laughter. Of the sunshine and the stars he sang, and the blue fury of the storm.

For the railroaders present, of the clanking side-rods and the booming exhaust as they drove their iron horse through daylight and dark, through the heat of summer and winter's icy grip, playing their part in the Winning of the West.

Of the Rio Grande and the men who dared its tawny flood. And for the girls of the dance floor and the girl who waited at the table, a poignantly beautiful song of love . . .

> ". . . winds that murmur softly
> Of a night of ecstasy.
> The brown leaves whisper,
> Couched where love has lain
> 'Neath the haunting purple fragrance
> Of wisteria in the rain!"

Returning the guitar to its owner, he sauntered back to the table amid a storm of applause that quivered the rafters.

There were tears on Carmen's dark lashes as she greeted him with a tremulous smile.

"You wrote that last one, did you not?" she asked.

To equivocate would have been unworthy. He simply answered, "Yes."

Fifteen

THE EVENING WORE ON, rowdy and gay, but with no trouble developing in the *cantina*. Deputy Caldwell dropped in to report that so far nothing of any consequence had taken place.

"The boys are whooping it up for fair, but everybody 'pears to be in a good temper, so far. A few wrangles are all we've had to contend with."

"Won't last," grunted the pessimistic sheriff. "Keep on your toes, and your eyes skun."

Caldwell promised to do so and sauntered out. A few minutes later Gordo Allendes glided in, caught Slade's eye, and shook his head, with an eloquent shrug of his shoulders. Evidently he'd had no luck.

"I see Pres Owen at the bar," the sheriff remarked. "I'm going over and have a few words with him. Maybe Gordo will have something to tell you." Slade nodded and beckoned the knifemen to join him.

Gordo sat down. The waiter poured wine, which Gordo tasted, signified approval. He spoke, his voice low.

"He neither I nor my *amigos* saw, and everywhere we looked," he said. "If in town is he, under cover he keeps."

"Which probably means he is either pulling something or planning to," Slade replied gloomily.

Events in the making would prove him no mean prophet relative to outlaw activities.

A sturdy little tug, the *Javelina*, plied the Rio Grande between Clint and El Paso, with contacts also with San Elizario, Socorro, Ysleta, and some ranches, the holdings of which extended to the river, the *Javelina* being in the nature of a "pick-up" conveyance.

Why it was named for a pig is anybody's guess. Perhaps because, like its porcine namesake, it had an omnivorous "appetite," its cargoes being heterogeneous. Hides, farm products, tools, machinery, and, at times, "other" things not advertised. Indulging, too, quite likely, in a little genteel smuggling now and then, which was regarded complacently along the border.

But the skipper, who was also the owner, was competent, square-shooting, and scrupulously honest. Reasons why he was entrusted with the "other" things when it was deemed the tug was safest transport.

In this particular instance, the other thing consisted of a large sum of money, the outcome of a deal between a land speculator and several farmers who desired to move elsewhere. It was consigned to the El Paso bank, and the expedient was supposed to be strictly secret. But as Slade said, the outlaw fraternity seemed able to learn what was not put out for public consumption.

Leaving the wharf that serviced Clint a couple of hours before midnight, the old tug chug-chugged cheerfully on its way to El Paso, not making much speed against the current, the river being rather high at the moment, but progressing steadily. Its paddles sent sparkles and ripples of silver across the moon-glowed stream.

The lights of San Elizario, Socorro, and Ysleta glittered, dropped behind. Another mile or so and on the north bank a lantern waved. The moonlight showed two horsemen sitting their saddles, beside them a heap of what appeared to be hides and baskets and boxes of farm produce.

It was a familiar sight to the pick-up, happened every few nights. The skipper acknowledged the signal with two short whistle blasts and turned the *Javelina*'s blunt nose toward the shore.

The tug bumped against the bank, hung stationary. The gangplank was lowered. The two horsemen, one tall, broad-shouldered, with a heavy dark beard, dismounted. Each shouldered a basket and trudged up the gangplank to where the skipper awaited them.

As they reached the deck, from a nearby clump of growth rode four more horsemen. The skipper glanced at them inquiringly, turned back to the bearded man and his companion, and looked into the muzzle of a gun!

"Into your cabin," ordered the bearded man. "Move!"

The skipper moved, for he saw death in the bearded man's glittering pale eyes. The other four horsemen were now mounting the gangplank. Another moment and they were holding guns on the engineer and deck hands.

In a corner of the skipper's cabin stood an old iron safe. The bearded man gestured to it with his gun barrel and spoke a single word.

"Open!"

The trembling skipper obeyed, twirling the combination knob, swinging the door wide. The bearded man's companion transferred the contents to a canvas sack.

"I want to say—" the skipper began. The bearded man clipped the top of his shoulder with a bullet. He fell back against the safe with a howl of pain. The other outlaws fired a volley over the heads of the demoralized deck hands. Then, the bearded man bringing up the rear, they walked backwards down the gangplank and mounted their horses, the bearded man's eyes still fixed on the deck where the hands huddled, afraid to move. The outlaws rode into the brush and out of sight. The whole affair hadn't taken ten minutes.

With the raving skipper holding a handkerchief

to his bullet-creased shoulder, the tug got under way, chugging for El Paso with a wide open throttle.

Midnight came and went, and Pablo's *cantina* was still doing a roaring business, but with so far no serious trouble developing. Slade didn't think there would be; the crowd, while noisy and hilarious, was good-tempered and jovial. He had a suspicion that elsewhere it might be different.

Gordo strolled in, shook his head, drank a glass of wine, and strolled out again. Slade was growing increasingly uneasy and experiencing an unpleasant presentiment that something serious was somewhere under way. He tried to shake off the feeling, but it persisted. Abruptly he turned to the sheriff.

"What say we amble around a bit?" he suggested. "And drop in at Roony's."

"I'm in favor of it," Serby replied. "A breath of fresh air will do good after all this blasted smoke."

Carmen was on the floor. Slade waved to her, and her anxious eyes followed his progress to the swinging doors.

They had barely stepped outside before they realized that the sheriff's prediction of a wild night was amply justified. And as they shoved their way through the swirling throng on their way to Roony's, the pandemonium intensified.

Broad Texas Street was a fair simulacrum of a Bacchanalian revel or an atavistic saturnalia of stark elementals under an orbed moon. High-pitched feminine laughter blended with the guffaws of men, for now there were women on the street, girls from the dance floors who had slipped out with their partners, and others. Slade chuckled to note that staid businessmen and dignified matrons from the fashionable residences that were beginning to rise near the crumbling face of Comanche Peak appeared as imbued with the general spirit of hilarity as the dance floor girls and the young cowhands. Well, they had a right to some fun, too. A chance to forget *their* cares and problems for a while.

Admiring glances followed the tall ranger as he passed. Those who knew him greeted him by name, respectfully, and young cowhands and railroaders said to their girls, "That's Deputy Slade who saved the payroll money from the owlhoots. If it wasn't for him, we wouldn't be having this bust tonight."

Finally, after quite a bit of shoving and buffeting, they made it to Roony's, a hospitable madhouse, where they received a rousing wel-come.

"The boys are raising the roof for fair, but no trouble worth mentioning," Roony said as he conducted them to their reserved table. "Deputy Hall and a couple of the specials were in, and aside from a scuffle or two that meant little, they had nothing to report."

However, before long something would be reported.

The sheriff ordered a snort. Slade settled for coffee, which he sipped slowly, viewing the colorful scene with pleasure. He felt the Roony patrons were as much drunk on excitement as redeye. Serby grumbled about rumhole owners getting rich and endeavored to look disgruntled, but failed. Slade was convinced the old gent was thoroughly enjoying himself.

Suddenly the swinging doors flew open with a bang, and two men bulged in, one with a blood-stained handkerchief tied under his armpit and over the top of his shoulder. They were the skipper and the engineer of the tugboat *Javelina*, both well known to Serby. They bawled for the sheriff, spotted him, and ploughed their way through the crowd and to the table.

The story of the robbery came out with a rush. Serby swore vehemently. Slade sat silent until the skipper finished his gabble, then asked a question.

"And you figure they rode north?"

"I think so," the skipper answered. "Couldn't see 'em after they dived into the brush, but I'm sure I heard the horses' hoofs beating north. Of course they might have turned east or west on the trail, but I don't think so."

"To very likely circle around, reach the trail, and slip into town one or two at a time," Slade commented.

"Expect you're right," agreed the skipper. "I don't see as there is anything you fellers can do about it, but I figured you'd oughta know."

"You figured right," Slade said. "Can you describe them?"

"Not too well," the skipper admitted. "The big feller I figure was the head of the devils, who plugged my shoulder, was big and tall and had black whiskers growing almost up to his eyes. The others were smaller and didn't have whiskers. Had their hatbrims pulled down low, their neckerchiefs pulled up high; nothing much of their faces to be seen."

"And I'll wager the big man with the beard did *not* have his hatbrim pulled down, his neckerchief pulled up high. Right?"

"By gosh, that's so," agreed the skipper. "How in blazes did you guess it? And why did he do it that way?"

"So you would describe him as you did," Slade explained. "The beard, an excellent disguise, was false. Also, that is why he just creased your shoulder instead of drilling you dead center, which is more in line with his way of doing things, so that your attention would be focused on him to the exclusion of the others."

"By gosh, it sure sounds reasonable," the

156

skipper said, gazing wonderingly at *El Halcón*. Slade smiled slightly.

"All right, to the back room and let me have a look at that shoulder," he directed. "Doubt if it amounts to much, but best not to take chances. It should be cleansed and properly bandaged. Roony has everything needed."

"Okay," replied the skipper. "You stay with the sheriff, Jake," he told the engineer.

Now the place was really in an uproar, but the crowd parted to let them through to the back room, where Roony was already laying out medicants.

Very quickly Slade had the slight wound smeared with antiseptic salve and neatly bandaged.

"Feel better?" he asked.

"A lot," the skipper said. "And I'll feel even a lot more better if you fellers manage to run down those devils. I don't mind the loss of the money so much—I'm insured—but it riles me proper to have had such a thing done to me. Never happened before."

Which, Slade reflected, was one of the reasons why it happened this time and doubtless would again in the future. Never happened before, so of course it never would happen, with no adequate precautions taken to prevent it happening at any time.

When they left the back room, the engineer

157

was at the bar, regaling eager listeners with a vivid account of the outrage. The skipper, after thanking Slade warmly for his ministrations, elected to join him. Slade moved on to his table, where Gordo Allendes was now sitting with Sheriff Serby.

Without preamble, the knifeman said, "From the east he rode. I the trail watched and saw. He rode the streets slowly, looking through windows. To the Arcadia, the *cantina* of the *Señor* Wilfred he rode. Outside the door the *Señor* Wilfred stood, and waved his hand in greeting. The other halted his *caballo* and sat in the moonlight. They talked. What was said I could hear not. The *caballo* was to the rack hitched. They entered the *cantina* together. I came to *Capitán*, an *amigo* watches. Is it well?"

"It is very well," Slade replied. "Yes, you did fine. And I don't think anything more is to be expected from him this night, so call in your boys and go down to Pablo's and have some fun."

Smiling, he held out his hand, in which something crackled. Gordo grinned delightedly as he glimpsed the denomination of the crisp bill that was slipped into his hand. The sheriff chuckled and extended a big paw.

"You're supposed to shake hands with me, too," he reminded. "And tell your boys hello for me."

Gordo grinned again, delightedly. "*Gracias, Capitán! Gracias, Señor* Sheriff!" he said, bowing low, and slid out the door.

"Slipped him the *dinero* I took off those three hellions laid out in the office," the sheriff said to Slade. "Figure him and his *muchachos* can use it, and the county treasury won't miss it."

Slade nodded agreement. "They have earned it," he replied.

Serby shot him a keen glance, but asked no questions concerning the rather peculiar discourse by Gordo to which Slade had listened with such intense interest, for he knew *El Halcón* was not yet ready to talk.

"Now what?" he asked.

"Guess we'd better stroll down to Pablo's *cantina* and see how things are going there. Plenty of noise and horseplay here, but no indications of serious trouble."

Waving to Roony, they set out, again shouldering their way through the uproarious throng. Without untoward happening, they reached Pablo's, which was also gay and noisy and, so far, peaceful.

Carmen joined them at once. "Of course we heard about the tugboat robbery," she said. "Thank goodness you didn't somehow manage to get mixed up in that. Really, my dear, you are on your good behavior tonight; I'm proud of you. I'll have to hustle back to the floor. Heavens!

What a night! And we won't get to close until after daylight. Oh well, happens only once a month, so I suppose I shouldn't complain."

"And you know very well you are enjoying every minute," Slade declared. She wrinkled her nose at him and flounced off to the floor. Slade laughed and ordered a cup of coffee to keep company with the sheriff's helping of red-eye.

An hour and a little more passed, with no letup of the hullabaloo. Then abruptly the doors swung open and Chet Wilfred, the Arcadia owner, entered. He paused, glanced about, located Slade and hurried to the table. He appeared to be laboring under suppressed excitement. He sat down, accepted a drink absently, gazed at the ranger for a moment, then broke into speech.

"Mr. Slade," he said, "you'll doubtless remember me telling you about seeing those seven wideloopers that night on the east-west trail?"

"Yes, I remember," Slade replied.

"And," continued Wilfred, "you will no doubt also recall me saying that the big tall fellow who appeared to be the leader of the bunch reminded me strongly of somebody, his build and his carriage. That I was sure I had seen somebody who greatly resembled him, but could not remember where or when. You asked me if I thought I would recognize him as that person did I see him again. And I said that if I could see the person under similar circumstances, sitting a horse in the moonlight, I believed I would."

He paused to sip his drink, still regarding *El Halcón* intently.

"Tonight," he concluded slowly, "I saw a certain person sitting a horse in the moonlight, and at once recognized him as the other man I saw that way before. I was utterly astounded. So much so that, although positive in my own mind, I really hesitate to call his name."

It was *El Halcón*, smiling slightly, who provided the name: *"Herman Gaunt!"*

The sheriff swore explosively. Wilfred's mouth dropped open; he stared, wide-eyed, at Slade. "You—you already knew Gaunt was the outlaw leader?" he gasped.

"I've known it for some time," the ranger replied composedly. "But unfortunately, I am still unable to prove it."

"But—but what I saw tonight—" Wilfred began.

"Is highly important, in that it corroborates my own deductions and belief," Slade interrupted. "But it does not make a case against Gaunt that would stand up in a court of law. A good lawyer would tear it to pieces with ease. And I have no intention of taking such a minor charge against Gaunt into court. What I want, and hope to have against him, is an airtight charge of murder that will stick."

"And which will be tried in Judge Colt's court, with a verdict against which there is no appeal," the sheriff interpolated dryly.

"Very likely," Slade agreed. "I doubt if he will ever be taken alive. And now, Mr. Wilfred, a word of advice to you, which you had better heed. Keep a tight *latigo* on your jaw. Don't mention to anybody what you told me tonight. If you do and Gaunt gets wind of it, your life will very likely not be worth a plugged peso. I only hope the cunning devil hasn't caught on that you have recognized him. While he was talking with you in your place tonight, did he ask what might be construed as deftly worded, probing questions?"

"I—I don't think so," Wilfred replied. "We just discussed the liquor business and ranching. I'm pretty sure that was all."

Slade hoped he was right. Anyhow there was another chore for Gordo and his knifemen—the chore of keeping Chet Wilfred alive.

Wilfred glanced at the clock, beckoned a waiter to serve a round of drinks.

"And then I'll have to get back to my place," he said. "Want to be there at closing time. And, Mr. Slade, I'll follow your advice to the letter. Concerning what you told me tonight, or relative to any other you see fit to give me. I'll admit," he added, with a wan smile, "that the way you said, you scared me a bit."

162

"Stay scared, and stay alive," the sheriff advised.

"I intend to," Wilfred replied. "Good night— good morning, rather. I'll be seeing you." With which he hurried out.

Carmen at once occupied the chair he had vacated. "I knew you three had something important to discuss, so I didn't intrude," she said.

"A beautiful woman never intrudes," the sheriff responded gallantly.

"Now who's been teaching *you* how to say pretty things?" Carmen retorted.

"Not that they aren't appreciated," she interrupted him, and flashed him a smile. "Well, it's daybreak, and I'm going to change. Been stepped on enough for one night." She whisked away to the dressing room.

In the east the dawn glowed scarlet and rose, with spears of golden light flaming to the zenith. A gentle breeze shook down myriad dew gems from the grass-heads. Birds chirped in the thickets, tried a tentative note or two, then, as the sun rose in splendor, burst into their chorus of homage to the King of Day!

Now El Paso's roar had died to a querulous mutter. The streets were deserted save for a few belated revellers staggering to their rest.

Once the *cantina* began thinning out, it emptied rapidly. The tired girls left the floor; the bartenders wiped away final drops of moisture; Pablo sounded his last call, and got little response, for which all the help was duly thankful.

The sheriff pushed back his empty glass, covered a yawn with a gnarled paw. Carmen glanced suggestively at Slade.

Sixteen

THE FOLLOWING AFTERNOON, the sheriff passed a hand across his aching brow and regarded Slade with envy.

"You and your coffee!" he moaned. "I'm ready to pass out, and you're fresh as a daisy. Coffee! But I gotta admit it doesn't make for a hangover. Someday, though, you're gonna turn into a blasted coffee bush."

"If you'd ever seen a coffee bush in bloom, you'd realize the high compliment you're paying me," Slade rejoined. "Really, there are few things as beautiful as a coffee bush in bloom. Snow crystals woven together with strands of moonlight. A field of coffee is a breathtaking sight."

"Oh, you'd see something purty in it, while I'd only see a bush," Serby grumbled.

"Yes," Slade agreed. "Were you set down in the Garden of Eden, you wouldn't have even seen Eve; too busy counting the scales on the snake."

"Safer to concentrate on the snake," Serby grinned. "But speaking of snakes, what's the really big project you mentioned Herman Gaunt has in mind, something bigger than widelooping cows and robbing tugboats?"

165

Slade sat silent for a few moments, gazing out the window at the flood of afternoon sunlight. Abruptly he appeared to have arrived at a decision.

"Trevis," he said, "let's take a little ride."

"Not a bad notion," replied the sheriff. "It is a nice day, and maybe the fresh air will blow some of the cobwebs outa my brain and get my think-tank into something like normal working order, bad as that is. Let's go. Doc don't figure to hold his inquest on those carcasses until after dark— got a case he has to look after earlier."

Without more ado they cinched up and set out. Slade turned east on the trail. Serby shot him a questioning glance but refrained from putting his thoughts into words. And *El Halcón*, continually scanning their surroundings with eyes that missed nothing, was silent until they reached the point where the river broke through the ridge that had formerly been its south bank, to circle the Mexican farmlands and put them in Texas. There he drew rein and sat regarding the tawny flood foaming down the slope.

"Trevis," he said, "why is Cordova Island still a part of Mexico, although lying north of the Rio Grande, the International Border?"

"Why, because it is the result of an artificial cut, made by mutual agreement, across the bend in the river."

Slade nodded, and gestured to the farmlands.

166

"While this, presumably made by a lightning bolt, is considered an act of God and not amenable to man-made laws."

"Guess that's so," Serby conceded.

"And were it proven that the cut in what was formerly the south bank of the river were man-made, the farmlands would still be part of Mexico despite the shift of the river. Right?"

"Right," the sheriff agreed. "But—"

"Well," Slade concluded. "As a matter of fact the cut was *not* made by a lightning bolt, but by dynamite planted by man. That being so, the farmlands are still a part of Mexico and owned by the Mexican farmers occupying them."

"For the love of Pete! Do you mean it?" sputtered Serby.

"I do," Slade repeated. "It is Herman Gaunt's big project I mentioned. Oh, he's a shrewd one, all right, and a first-rate engineer. He and his devils planted the dynamite in the ridge that was the south bank, waited until a night of storm with plenty of lightning and thunder to make the explosion seem to be just another thunderclap, set off the charge, and blew a gap in the ridge, which the river quickly widened and deepened."

"How in blazes did you catch onto it?" Serby wondered.

"Well, I also happen to be an engineer," Slade explained. "I knew that the gap in the ridge had never been made by a lightning bolt. Had one struck the ridge, highly unlikely, it would have just fluffed off the surface. Dynamite, to the contrary, when properly set and tamped, blows down. A sufficient quantity tore through the ridge from its crest to its base, and the river rushing into the gap did the rest. Beginning to understand?"

"Guess I am, the way you put it," Serby admitted. "But how did you tie it onto Gaunt?"

"To an extent, by a process of elimination," Slade replied. "When I saw the breakthrough I knew the contention it had been done by a lightning bolt was just so much sheepdip. I knew very well the course of the river had been altered by men, and I wondered why in the world anybody would do such a thing. But when you mentioned that somebody had gotten an option on the farmlands almost the day they were shifted from Mexico to the north of the Rio Grande and presumedly became Texas State land, the reason was obvious."

"Uh-huh, obvious to you," the sheriff interrupted. "Nobody else ever thought of it, and the chances are, never would have."

"Possibly," Slade conceded, and continued. "Realizing that the spade work had been done for a gigantic steal, I at once started browsing around in an endeavor to spot somebody with the necessary engineering and hydraulic knowledge to concoct such a scheme and put it into effect. I was confident it was a newcomer to the section, which greatly narrowed the search. Your *amigo* Chet Wilfred looked a mite promising for a while, but I quickly discarded him. He just didn't fit into the picture. As a possible widelooper or robber, yes, but not as a farsighted geological genius of unusual ability plus unusual imagination."

"And Gaunt did," the sheriff interpolated.

"Yes, after I got to really thinking about him," Slade answered. "After certain incidentals convinced me definitely that he was the head of the outlaw bunch. He is shrewd, able, and adroit, but he makes the little slips the outlaw brand seems always prone to make. Always right before a try to kill me was made he was in evidence, even asking about me. Why should he be so interested in me and my movements? Because, as I quickly concluded, he had spotted me as *El Halcón* with a reputation for horning into good things other people had started or contemplated and considered me a menace to his plans."

"Sounds plumb reasonable," the sheriff commented.

"And that member of his bunch disguised as a brother to whom he handed the chore of eliminating me made a very bad slip when he hung onto the unused percussion caps after exploding the dynamite that changed the course of the river. That definitely tied up the outlaw

169

bunch with the farmlands project, Gaunt's big objective, against which he was amassing money by way of his widelooping, robbing, and so forth. And it was not long until I had decided Gaunt was one of the outlaws, presumably the head of the pack."

Slade paused to roll and light a cigarette. When the smoke was going to his satisfaction, he continued.

"As you have often heard me say, a man can change the color of his hair, his complexion, can don a false beard that can't be detected from the real thing, but he cannot change his build or his carriage, and Herman Gaunt's build and carriage are distinctive, striking to an extent not often met with. And no matter what disguise he adopted, he could not change them. And as it happened I got a few pretty good looks at him in his outlaw role. During the attempted widelooping of Judson's cows, and the try at the railroad payroll money, for instance.

"So, convinced in my own mind, I sent a wire to my friend in the Land Office, asking who held the option on the farmlands. The answer came back in two words that spelled a name:

" *'Herman Gaunt!'*

"And there you are."

"Well, you sure make out a case against the sidewinder," the sheriff said.

"Yes," Slade replied smilingly, "only I fear it

is like unto the house built on the sand, of which we are told in the Scriptures."

"How's that?" wondered Serby.

Slade quoted,

" 'And the rain descended, and the floods came, and the winds blew, and beat upon that house; and it fell . . .' For it was built on the sand.

"And that's the way with my case against Gaunt. It is foundationed on the sands of theory, conjecture, and supposition. One good 'puff' by a smart lawyer, and down it would go!"

"Hmmm!" the sheriff remarked reflectively. "Seems to me that story also had to do with a smart jigger who built his house on a rock and told the wind and the rain and the waters to do their darndest. That's the kind of a case you'll end up building against the horned toad."

"Hope you're right," Slade smiled. "That it is built on the 'rock' of undeniable fact."

"My money's on *El Halcón*," Serby said. "By the way, do you figure Wilfred will manage to keep Gaunt from catching on that he's recognized him as an outlaw?"

"Unless something riles him and causes him to fly off the handle and say things he shouldn't," Slade replied. "For he's got a flashy temper and is impulsive. That must be taken into consideration."

"Maybe it might be a good thing if they got

together," Serby remarked cheerfully. "Wilfred might take care of the blasted wind spider."

"Small chance," Slade differed. "Chet is a salty *hombre*, all right, and capable, but compared to Herman Gaunt, he's just a little wooly lamb."

The farmers had spotted them sitting their horses on the crest of the slope, and beckoned.

"What say we amble down for a jabber with them?" Serby suggested.

"Not a bad idea," Slade agreed. They put their horses to the slope.

When they reached the level ground, the old head man of the farmers bowed low to *El Halcón*, shook hands with the sheriff, and insisted they have a glass of wine and a bite to eat with him.

The invitation was accepted and they sat down to a tasty repast.

"The *Señor* Judson visited us," remarked the head man. "A fine *hombre*."

"Yes, he is," Slade agreed. "And a good *amigo*. When he's your friend, he's your friend all the way. Incidentally, he packs plenty of influence with the ranchers of the section, and he's putting in a word for you fellows where it counts most."

"And the word that *El Halcón* put in with the *Señor* Judson counted much with him," said the head man with a smile.

Several more farmers dropped in, and they had quite a party. The lower edge of the sun was touching the horizon when Slade and the sheriff rode up the slope and headed for town through the soft hush of the dying day, with the shadows curdling under the chaparral.

As had often happened in the past, it was Slade's eyes that saved them from disaster. Suddenly he saw a flash of light on the brush-grown crest of a rise a thousand yards or so to the front. A flash that could only have come from shifted metal reflecting the flame of the sunset.

"Trevis," he said, "looks like we're riding into a nice sociable drygulching. But with a little luck we may be able to turn the tables on those enterprising gents holed up on that hill crest ahead."

"What—what!" exclaimed the sheriff. "How do you know?" Slade told him.

"Do you ever miss anything?" groaned Serby. "How do you plan to handle it?"

"I've been expecting something like this ever since the first time I rode down this way and have carefully studied the terrain," Slade explained. "That ridge crest commands the trail, and of course the open prairie to the north. But to the south of the rise, where the river veers slightly to the south, is a strip between the brush and the water's edge that can be ridden. The devils holed up on that rise will be concentrating on the trail, with no reason to pay particular attention to the south of the rise, or so I figure it. In fact, I consider it rather doubtful that they can view that stretch of beach. Anyhow, we'll take a chance on it and see if we can't slide along that way, ease up the rise and, with a little luck, take the gents in the rear. Worth trying, don't you think?"

"I sure do," growled Serby. "May be taking a bit of a risk, but what the heck! What's the first move?"

"They can't see us yet, so right here we turn south through the brush," Slade answered. They put the horses to the growth.

The cayuses didn't particularly favor it but offered no serious objections. In due time, they came out on the little strip of beach that edged the river for a mile or so upstream. Crowding close to the chaparral, where the shadows were already deepening, they continued cautiously, Slade drawing rein now and then to peer and listen.

"So far no indications of the sidewinders suspecting something out of order," he said. "A couple of hundred yards more and we'll leave the bronks in the brush and slide along and up the rise on foot."

A few more moments of slow pacing and they dismounted, shoved the horses into the brush again, and stole along until Slade once more halted. Overhead the sunset colors were fading. Another twenty minutes and it would be quite dark under the chaparral.

"Which should work to our advantage," Slade

breathed. "We will know exactly what we want to do, while they should be caught off balance. Hope we're not too badly outnumbered."

"We won't be for long," the sheriff predicted grimly in a whisper. "Where those snakes are concerned, I'm feeling like Gordo and his thirsty blade. We'll even the score in a hurry." Slade suppressed a grin, and led the way into the growth.

The slope was rather steep, but the chaparral not heavy enough to provide serious difficulty to experienced foresters. Step by step they eased along, reached the flat crest, a few yards in width.

Abruptly Slade laid a restraining hand on the sheriff's shoulder; to his ears had come the sound of low voices, a querulous mutter. He couldn't quite catch what was said; different voices registered.

"I think there are four of them," he breathed. "Come along, I want to make sure."

Cautiously, silently, they crept forward, until they were almost to the beginning of the northern downward slope. Slade was endeavoring to maneuver them into a position from which they could see the drygulchers without being seen by them. Another moment and they were at the final straggle of growth before the slope, and Slade made out the shadowy forms of four dry-gulchers, gazing eastward along the trail below, all set to do murder. His jaw set grimly, his eyes were icy-cold. And a most unexpected diversion occurred.

From the west, no great distance away, came a crackle of gunfire!

Seventeen

"WHAT IN BLAZES!" gasped the sheriff.

Slade was equally astonished, and so, it appeared, were the four drygulchers, judging from the storm of exclamations that arose from their ranks.

Recklessly, Slade pushed forward through the final straggle of growth until he had a view of the trail.

Around a bend a couple of hundred yards to the west bulged five horsemen, going like the wind, shooting over their shoulders. Around the bend some fifty yards to the rear of the first bunch boomed a second group, numbering more than half a dozen, also shooting, their target the five to the front.

"Good gosh!" the sheriff barked at what Slade had already noted. "That second bunch is Sime Judson's Tumbling J hands!"

And the four drygulchers had evidently recognized the first bunch, for they leaped out of the straggle, yelling to them.

The first bunch swerved their horses into the growth and came boiling up the slope, and Slade instantly saw there was something that had to be taken care of at once. The four drygulchers were lining sights with the Tumbling J hands!

"Hold it! Get your hands up! You're covered!" his great voice rolled in thunder.

The drygulchers whirled at the sound of his voice, guns jutting to the front. Slade hurled the sheriff back into the straggle and went sideways and down in the same flicker of movement, whipping out both Colts.

Back and forth through the fading twilight gushed the orange flashes. And a bellowing echo were the blazing Tumbling J guns as the cowboys stormed up the slope in pursuit of their fleeing quarry.

Bullets hummed past Slade like angry hornets, ripped his shirtsleeve and the leg of his overalls, drilled a hole through the crown of his hat. But two drygulchers fell before the booming Colts. A third went down as Serby also cut loose with both hands. Into view flashed the fleeing outlaws, only three of them now, with the cowboys whooping their triumph and shooting as fast as they could squeeze trigger.

Slade and the remaining drygulcher fired together. *El Halcón* reeled slightly as a slug just touched his temple. But the drygulcher crumpled up like a sack of old clothes and lay motionless beside his dead companions.

Halfway down the south slope, the Tumbling J cowhands were chattering and laughing. Evidently they had come out top dog in their ruckus with the fleeing outlaws.

Slade's voice rolled down the slope.

"Come on up here and tell the sheriff how you managed to mix into this shindig."

"Be right up, Mr. Slade, don't gun us," was the whooped reply.

"Talk about a corpse-and-cartridge session!" marveled Serby. "There ain't been this much powder burned in Texas since the battle of Resaca Palms! Gentlemen, tip your hats!"

The Tumbling J hands streamed into view. In answer to Slade's question, the range boss explained how they came to be chasing the outlaw bunch.

"We were heading for town," he said. "Some of the boys who were on patrol didn't get to go in for payday, so we were ambling in to give them a chance to have a little fun. We were cutting across the range, rounded a clump of brush and saw those five hellions rounding up a bunch of cows beside a waterhole. When they saw us coming, they hightailed. We sifted sand after 'em. You saw what else happened."

"And if it wasn't for Walt spotting those four drygulchers lining sights with you, you mighty likely wouldn't be telling us about it," said Serby, and explained what he meant by *that*.

As a result, the Tumbling J bunch, one and all, solemnly shook hands with Slade.

" 'Pears he's always getting everybody plumb deep in debt to him," sighed the range boss.

"And that you can say four or five times," said the sheriff.

Slade changed the subject by inquiring if anybody was hurt.

"Oh, a couple of nicks is all," replied the range boss. "Toby has a hunk of meat knocked outa his cheek; nothing to bother about. Jack Rawlins has a bullet cut in his arm, Watson a punctured leg. Guess the hellions were caught plumb off-balance. Sure shot that way."

Slade whistled Shadow, secured his medicants and got busy on the minor wounds, a couple of dry sotol stalks providing enough light to work by. Antiseptic ointment, pads and bandages were applied.

"That should hold you until the doctor looks you over," he told the sufferers, who didn't appear to be suffering to an extent that a shot or two of redeye wouldn't alleviate.

Meanwhile, the range boss had located the horses ridden by the four drygulchers, tethered to nearby trees. The rigs were stripped off and they were turned loose to fend for themselves for the time being.

"The others are to hell and gone in the brush," said the range boss. "When we leave here I'll ride to the *casa* and tell Sime what happened. He'll arrange to have the cayuses run down tomorrow."

"And we'll need daylight to root out the carcasses," said the sheriff. "Guess *they* can make out where they are. One thing is sure for certain: they ain't going anywhere."

Slade examined the four drygulchers, giving particular attention to their hands.

"Two had been cowhands quite a while back; the other two something else," he announced.

"More river pirates, eh?" growled Serby. "They look it." Slade thought he was probably right.

"And the nerve of those other devils!" Serby added. "Staging a widelooping in broad daylight."

"An example of the shrewd thinking on the part of our *amigo* who is head of the pack," Slade replied. "The day after payday, with everybody concentrating on getting over the effects of the celebration, the range deserted, and the night patrols not yet on duty. Just a fluky chance that it wasn't successful, due to the unexpected decision of the range boss and the others, riding to town to give those who missed out on the payday bust a chance for a little recreation."

"Well," observed the sheriff, "looks to me like today's ruckus must have just about wiped out his bunch, wouldn't you say?"

"One would think so," Slade conceded, "but we can't be sure. And he can get more, if he feels the need of them."

"Section's crawling with 'em," grunted Serby. "Well, everything 'pears to be under control here, so how about heading for town? I'm beginning to feel lank again, after all the excitement."

"Guess we might as well," Slade agreed. "Grab off your cayuse and we'll get going."

With the cowhands still chattering excitedly, the wounded making light of their hurts, they set out, riding at a good pace, and before long the lights of El Paso twinkled into view.

"Not such a bad day after all, although it looked a mite scary when those devils turned on us," Serby said. "Much obliged for taking time and risking your own life to shove me into the brush. Chances are it saved me from getting nicked."

"I had to get you out of my way," Slade smiled. Serby snorted, but refrained from arguing the point.

Reaching town, Slade and the sheriff cared for their horses and then repaired to Roony's for a surrounding, of which they were both in need.

When they arrived, the Tumbling J hands were already there, and greeted them with joyous whoops. They were evidently giving a lurid account of the afternoon's stirring happenings, in which Slade figured prominently.

"Shut up!" Slade told them. "We want to eat in peace."

The order was not obeyed, but Roony and his floor men did manage to shoo them away from the table while the two peace officers were putting away their surrounding. And by the time they had finished, the drinks and the girls had taken over, and they were let alone.

The sheriff pushed back his empty plate, called for a snort of redeye as a chaser. Slade settled for another cup of steaming coffee and manufactured a cigarette.

"I can't get over the way you spotted those blankety-blank drygulchers," Serby remarked. "Just don't seem possible."

"Light reflected from the metal of a nickel-finish gun can be seen for a great distance," Slade replied.

"Uh-huh, by eyes like yours," the sheriff said.

"Even your eyes would have noted it had you been looking in that direction, with your mind on such matters," Slade answered. "Another one of the little slips the outlaw fraternity seem always prone to make; they overlook trifles and their significance. In this case the slip, small though it was, proved fatal."

"I reckon you're right," sighed the sheriff. "You always seem to be. Sure were in this instance."

"If there is anything the ranger 'book' bears down on it is the importance of trifles," Slade pointed out. "Just a matter of training."

"Uh-huh, the *El Halcón* sort of training," said the sheriff. "Oh, well, we'll let go at that and thank Pete it is so. I still get the creeps, thinking of what might have happened. Now what's the line-up?"

"I think we'd better amble down to Pablo's *cantina*," Slade replied. "He or Gordo might have something to tell us. Don't want to pass up any bets."

"You're darn right," growled Serby. "Say! the word of what happened sure got around fast. The darn rumhole is packed with folks wanting to hear about it. And they're beginning to look this way."

"Come on, let's get out of here," Slade said, rising to his feet.

The sheriff chuckled and followed the ranger to the swinging doors.

"A darn shame Gaunt wasn't with that bunch of wideloopers," he remarked. "That would have made it perfect. I suppose he's somewhere cookin' up some deviltry of his own."

"Quite likely," Slade replied. "Today's attempts were routine chores he passed on to the hired hands. In which he made a slip."

"About one more will be his last," predicted the sheriff. "I'm ready to bet on that."

"We'll trust you are right," Slade replied.

Without incident, they reached the *cantina*, where Carmen and Pablo were impatiently awaiting them.

"We heard something: guess most of the town did," the girl said. "We gathered from the reports brought in that you had just about decimated El Paso County, but thought that was probably a slight exaggeration. However, seeing as you were back in town safe, we didn't worry too much. Let's have the straight of it."

The sheriff obliged, in detail, listened to intently by his hearers.

"Yep, it was quite a go," he concluded. "A regular lead pushing for fair. I never saw a livelier. Can still smell the powder."

"Well, you came back safe, and that's all that really counts," said Carmen. "Perhaps we can have a peaceful night for a change, even though we have an unusually large crowd for the day after payday. I think Walt inspires folks and they all want to have a look at him and hear what he has to say. Don't grumble, my dear; the penalty you have to pay for being famous."

The night did jog along peacefully, the *cantina* gay and lively but with no trouble. Slade and Carmen had several dances together. He chatted with the cook and the kitchen help. Gordo dropped in with nothing to report. A while later the Tumbling J range boss also dropped in.

"As soon as it gets light, Sime and the boys will comb the brush for those outlaw carcasses and load 'em into a wagon for delivery at your office, Trevis," he said.

"That will help," replied the sheriff. "Much obliged. One of my deputies will be there if I don't happen to rouse up that early. He'll take care of them."

"Guess they're pretty well took care of already," chuckled the range boss, with grisly humor, Carmen thought. The hours passed, the crowd thinned out. Carmen changed to a street dress.

"A new rose bush is in full bloom, very beautiful," she said.

"And I know from whence it filched its beauty," Slade replied, smilingly.

The sheriff chuckled, and glanced at the clock.

Eighteen

THE FOLLOWING AFTERNOON, Serby eyed the office floor with a complacent and pleased expression.

"Now that's something like," he said to Slade, jerking his head toward the nine blanketed forms. "Old Sime didn't overlook any and had 'em all here before noon, Deputy Hall told me. Rounded up all the horses, too; good-looking critters. Some of 'em have Mexican skillet-of-snakes brands, the others what I figure to be New Mexico or east Arizona slick-ironed burns. Maybe you can make something of them."

"Quite unlikely," Slade replied. "Altered brands, of course, and tracing a horse back to its origin is difficult, and usually nothing attained by so doing. Horses can be sold, traded, stolen, and show up a long way from where they were foaled."

"Guess that's so," the sheriff conceded. "Well, we've got the riders, and I reckon that's the important thing. Doc will hold an inquest later and then we'll plant 'em. Pockets turned out quite a bit of *dinero*, but nothing else of importance, so far as I can ascertain; the junk is over there on the table."

187

Slade examined the heap of odds and ends, mostly the trinkets range riders usually pack with them, and agreed with Serby that there was nothing of importance.

"What is important to us is where, and when, Gaunt is going to strike next," he observed.

"Think he's got anybody much left to strike with?" asked the sheriff.

"Very likely some of his key men he didn't use for a genteel drygulching or running off a few stolen beefs," was Slade's opinion. "I figure he still needs to amass a bit more money to take up his option on the farmlands. I may be wrong in that, but somehow I don't believe I am. I fear he'll be out for something big. What? Right now I haven't the slightest idea."

"Set one of your hunches to working," was Serby's cheerful advice.

"Set a hunch to catch a bunch, eh?" Slade laughed. "Maybe it'll work. Well, I'm going to amble down to the *cantina* after a bit and find out if Gordo has learned anything."

"How about knocking off a snack at Roony's first?" Serby suggested. "Being in a hurry to get here, I haven't had any breakfast."

"Same goes for me," Slade answered. "I can use a helping about now."

Serby locked the door and they made their way to the saloon. Business was slack, the hour being early, so they ate a leisurely meal without interruption. They had finished their repast and were enjoying a final snort, cup of coffee, smoke, when Doc McChesney strolled in.

"Done got a jury lined up and will set on those carcasses whenever it is okay with you, Trevis," he said.

"Sooner the quicker, so let's get it over with," the sheriff replied. "Want the hellions planted soon as possible; getting sorta ripe in this warm weather."

"Right you are," said Doc. "The Tumbling J hands stayed over for the inquest, of course, and I've got them lined up, too."

"Let's go," said Serby, shoving aside his empty glass.

With all the Tumbling J hands, still pretty well under the influence of redeye, wanting to get in on the act, the inquest was a rather long affair. The jury's verdict, of course, a foregone conclusion, exonerated everybody of blame. Plant 'em and forget 'em!

Quite a few individuals, including several of the jury, recalled seeing one or more of the slain outlaws in the bars or on the streets, but remembered nothing significant concerning them.

To which Slade gave scant thought. He knew his man, and that was all that really counted. Belatedly, quite belatedly, he and the sheriff headed for Pablo's *cantina*.

Gordo was lounging at the end of the bar when

they entered. Slade paused for a word with him.

"In town he rode," said the knifeman, referring to Herman Gaunt. "In the *cantina* he had the drink with Pablo. Then north he rode. I, of course, could not follow."

"Would have been unwise to do so," Slade said. "Well, I doubt he will return to town tonight, but have your boys keep an eye out, just in case."

"That I will do," promised Gordo. Slade joined the sheriff at their table.

"What in blazes could he be headed for to the north?" wondered the sheriff when the information was relayed to him.

"Well, for one thing there's the north trail, which runs through the Hueco Mountains by way of Hueco Pass, past the Guadalupe Mountains, and traverses Texas for about a hundred miles, with cow factories and so forth lining the way. The gentleman can just about take his pick.

"And I can't help wondering," Slade continued thoughtfully, "if they mightn't have a hole-up somewhere to the north. It is rather logical to believe they have one; usually the way with such gentry. A place where they can lie low for a while if things get a bit hot, or get together to divide the loot."

"Maybe in the Huecos, say around the Hueco Tanks section," suggested Serby. "Once before sort of hit paydirt there. Liable to run onto anything in that upended section of hell."

The Hueco Tanks, about six miles to the north of the trail, was of historical and archaeological interest to Slade. In a section a mile long and better than half a mile wide, a great clutter of giant rocks lay scattered in wild confusion. In this natural fortress, various tribes, from prehistoric men to the era of the Hueco-section occupation by the Apache Indians, had villages secure from attack by hostile bands. Erosion had cut numerous waterholes in the soft granite in which rainwater was retained, in many cases remaining pure and sweet.

Shallow caves and narrow overhung canyons offered protection from wind and storms. With far back among the roughest and highest rock formations the largest, most difficult to reach "tank," where there was always a pool of crystal-clear water.

Slade made it a habit to visit the area if possible whenever he happened to be in the section. In addition to his scientific interest, he knew that more than one outlaw bunch had found temporary, at least, sanctuary in the region, holed up in a cave or twisty canyon and fairly safe from detection. History might repeat. He ordered more coffee and sat gazing out the window.

The sheriff stuffed his pipe and puffed contentedly. He knew *El Halcón* was tracing something up and down the corridors of his mind, and visioned more blanketed forms on his office floor.

Carmen bounced over the floor and plumped into a chair beside Slade, regarding him accusingly.

"I know that look," she said. "Something's building up, trouble for somebody, with me gnawing my nails again."

"Could be," Slade smiled. "But I ventured to predict it won't be tonight, not with all those new roses in bloom."

Carmen slanted him a glance through her lashes, wrinkled her nose at the sheriff's sly chuckle.

"Let's dance," she said, and led the way to the floor.

" 'Gather ye rosebuds while ye may,' " she quoted softly as they fell into position. " 'And with them, bright, glorious, wonderful, with a laugh for the past and a jest for the future, strode the Spirit of Youth!' "

After the amount of thought he had expended upon it the night before, it appeared not at all remarkable that early morning would find Walt Slade riding east on the north trail that ran through Hueco Pass.

However, his destination was not the Huecos, although he followed the trail for perhaps a half-
ı miles. In the shadow of a clump of thicket

that fringed the trail on the north, he drew rein and for quite a while sat studying the back trail.

"Well, horse," he finally said, "here's where we play another hunch, a sort of *loco*-appearing one on the surface, but it does deal with something that it seems nobody in the section has thought of. So we'll take a chance and hope for results."

With which he turned Shadow's nose and rode due north. For several miles he rode through a desolate region, then turned west no great distance from the New Mexico Territory line, riding rather slowly and watchfully.

Even in the bright sunshine, the area had a lonely and forbidding look, this no-man's land between territory and state. The voices of the birds, usually so musically cheerful, were hesitant, subdued. And the few little brush animals Slade saw scurried in and out of the growth furtively, with a very dubious eye for the lone horseman. A land that even the outlaw shunned, as a rule. But, *El Halcón* believed, not always.

And as he rode, the bare, craggy peaks of the Franklin Mountains, north of El Paso, steadily drew nearer. And the grim austerity of the Franklins was his goal.

Shadow snorted disapprovingly as he viewed the prospect, causing his rider to chuckle.

"And no matter what you say, the hunch is growing stronger," Slade told him. "It's never been done before, so of course it never will be done. A nice, comforting delusion, but things don't always work out in such a desirable fashion. So I'm playing my hunch that this is the exception that proves the rule. June along, horse, and we'll judge all this for ourselves."

Shadow apparently didn't think the monologue worthy of comment and jogged along unconcernedly toward the somber network of canyons and gorges, with no westward pass through the tangle. Soon the beat of his irons echoed back from the towering peaks, seven thousand feet and more in height, and the gloom of the foothills enveloped horse and rider.

Once again Slade halted his mount and for some minutes sat gazing back the way he had come, a vista of sunshine and peace. Then, with a shrug of his broad shoulders, he faced to the front and the darksome prospect ahead and began his toilsome search.

Hour after hour he combed canyons and gorges, the majority of them narrow, all boxed, and discovered nothing. Finally he sent Shadow up a rocky incline that appeared to level off quite a distance above, from where he hoped to gain a more comprehensive view of the terrain. Shadow made it to the crest without too much difficulty, and Slade rode along the lip of a beetling cliff, with white water foaming and brawling hundreds of feet below.

From the elevated position, he could see, to the west, another and very narrow canyon which it appeared could be entered from the level ground at the base of the slope.

"And somehow, horse, I've a feeling that crack looks promising," he told Shadow. "Just why I feel that way, I don't know, but I do. I believe we have time to give it a once-over before night settles down and it'll be black dark in this hell's half-acre. Let's go!"

As he expected, he experienced no difficulty reaching the mouth of the canyon. It proved to be very narrow and somewhat twisty, with but a scanty stand of low brush bristling up from its floor.

A few moments after he turned into it, his pulses quickened exultantly. There was indubitable evidence that cattle had passed up the gorge no great time before. Evidence, also, that they had been run in from time to time.

Now *El Halcón* rode with every sense at hairtrigger alertness, for there was no telling what he might run into, and the narrow canyon with its low and scanty chaparral growth provided no concealment. The gorge was already growing gloomy, although the sun had not yet set, but his curiosity was at white heat and he felt he couldn't seek the outer air until he had explored this sinister crack in the mountains to its depths.

He had covered perhaps a mile and a half when

he rounded one of the turns and before him was the explanation of the cattle stolen from the northern pastures, always a few at a time, with the wrathful owners glowering suspiciously at the Rio Grande, combing the Huecos and other likely spots in search of their purloined beefs and finding nothing!

As Slade was positive it would be, the canyon was a box, the end wall a beetling cliff a hundred and more feet in height, so grown with vines and trailing creepers from crest to base that little of the dark stone was visible.

The cliff was not perpendicular but sloped back at a sharp angle, and built where end and side wall joined was a rough but serviceable corral. It was empty at the moment, but showed the signs of occupancy from time to time by many head of cattle.

"Yes, feller, we played a straight hunch," Slade told the horse. "Right here, almost in El Paso's back yard, is where the widelooped cattle are holed up, little bunches at a time, until a sizable herd is ready for the New Mexico buyers. So darn simple, and so darn clever. *Amigo* Gaunt is a genius in more ways than one. Well, we'll see."

Slade had noted something else that intrigued his curiosity and birthed an uneasy concern, a lingering tang of wood smoke. But there was no cabin or shack in the canyon that might have provided a hole-up for men, and no indications that outdoor fires had been kindled anywhere in the vicinity.

"Something funny about it, feller," he told Shadow. "But we'd better not risk further investigation at this time. If the hellions happen to be headed this way and we meet them in this narrow slit with no cover, we quite likely wouldn't enjoy the encounter. So let's get going out of here.

"And incidentally, horse," he added, "I'm of the opinion that there *is* a hole-up here, and I'm getting a notion as to where it is. We'll put that to the test, but not today."

He experienced a sense of relief when he debouched from the canyon and turned east. Soon he would be in a position to make a straight shoot to the north trail and El Paso.

"And the nosebag, feller," he said. "Which we're both in need of." Shadow, sensing oats in the offing, stepped out briskly.

They had almost reached the point where they would turn south when wafted on a breeze blowing up from the south came a sound, a staccato sound as of thorns burning briskly under a pot.

But *El Halcón* knew it was nothing that innocent. Without a doubt it was a blast of gunfire, and gunfire in this region usually meant trouble.

In this particular instance it certainly did.

Nineteen

THE STAGE from Alamogordo, New Mexico, to El Paso was not as imposing an equipage as the great Butterfield coaches that formerly rolled through Hueco Pass on their way to California, but nevertheless was a going concern, servicing as it did a number of small New Mexico communities.

Also, in Alamogordo was an outlet for the costly jewelry, rare perfumes, and souvenirs of Aztec art that were transported north via the stage to be transshipped to all parts of the country, and abroad.

In consequence, the southbound stage often carried a large sum of money, the Mexican vendors preferring cash to checks.

Leaving Alamogordo in the early morning, the stage laid over for the night at Orogrande, New Mexico, and resumed its journey the following morning.

So the whole run was made by daylight.

The stage had never been held up. The terrain over which it passed was not favorable for a robbery attempt, the route being almost entirely across open prairies, where the driver and the outside rifle guard could see for miles in every direction.

In addition, there was a second guard inside the coach. The walls were thick, the windows were narrow and barred, and both doors were locked.

And the guards were salty oldtimers, shrewd, experienced, and dead shots. All in all, the Alamogordo stage was not a good outlaw prospect.

Late afternoon, and now the stage had but a few more miles to go, across the Texas prairie, then the north trail and El Paso. The stage crew relaxed comfortably. The coach careened around a narrow straggle of growth and came upon a familiar scene, especially at this time of the year.

A small fire had been kindled, its smoke wavering on the breeze blowing up gently from the south. A bearded man in rangeland clothes was heating a branding iron in the fire. Two more men were holding the legs of a calf stretched on its side and complaining bitterly. A fourth cowboy—at least he looked like one—held taut a rope around the calf's neck. Four patient horses stood nearby.

Yes, a familiar scene, cowhands at work. The man manipulating the branding iron glanced up as the stage drew abreast of the operation, waved in answer to the driver's wave, and turned back to his work. A bawl of pain from the calf as the iron was applied. The stage swept on. Neither driver nor outside guard noted that each "cowhand" had a rifle hidden in the long grass where he crouched.

The outside guard never did note it. He spun from the high seat with a bullet through his heart as the rifles blazed. The driver also fell, to lie motionless beside the dead guard. Smoke puffed from the coach as the inside guard tried to fight back. Slugs hammered the coach, screeched through the narrow windows. There was a gurgling cry, then silence inside the coach.

The four pseudo-cowhands dashed to the coach, rifles ready. One caught the bewildered horses and brought the vehicle to a halt. A slug smashed the lock, the door swung open. The inside guard's body was shoved aside, a plump money pouch hauled out.

"This is it," said the bearded leader of the robbers. "Let's go!"

All four sped to where their horses stood beside the smoldering fire, swung into the hulls and raced east.

The stage driver was not dead. A crafty old-timer, shot through the shoulder and hurled from the seat, he knew his only chance was to play 'possum and hope the killers would not notice the deception. Bleeding profusely, he lay perfectly still, scarce daring to breathe, and saw the outlaws vanish into the east. Struggling to a sitting position, he strove to stanch the bleeding that was fast draining away his strength, with little success. With a sobbing moan he slumped forward as to his dimming ears came the sound of fast hoofbeats approaching.

For a moment after hearing that continued, ominous crackle of gunfire, Slade sat tense in the saddle, listening. Then his voice rang out, "Trail, Shadow, trail!"

The great black lunged forward and almost instantly was going like the wind, responding gallantly to Slade's urging for speed and more speed. In an amazingly short time he reached the point where his master had a clear view south across the open prairie.

Leaning forward in the hull, peering ahead, Slade spotted the motionless stage with a still form lying beside it, another crouched in the grass. With Shadow going at full speed, he left the saddle, rocked back on his heels, reeled, caught his balance. A single glance told him there was not a moment to spare if the driver's life was to be saved. He whipped out his medicants and knelt beside the wounded man, talking soothingly to him the while. Working at top speed, he smeared the injury with antiseptic ointment, padded it heavily, noting with satisfaction that the bleeding was already slackening. Another pad, a careful pressure of his thumb in exactly the right spot, still another pad, and he saw the pulse of blood had almost ceased. Deftly he bandaged the pads securely in place.

"Feel better?" he asked.

"A helluva lot," the driver panted. "Thought I was a goner. Guess I would have been if you hadn't come along." Slade didn't argue the point.

"Say! I know you," the driver exclaimed. "You're Mr. Slade, Sheriff Serby's deputy, right?"

"Yes," Slade replied. "Think you can tell me just what happened?"

The driver proceeded to do so, so far as he knew. Slade glanced at the smoldering fire and nodded.

"Very clever," he said. "A brand new wrinkle; never heard of the like. Calculated to fool anybody."

"It sure fooled us," the driver sighed. "And cost two lives."

"And they rode east?"

"That's right. Guess they were out of sight by the time you got here."

"Can you describe them?"

"Not too well," the driver admitted. "One who 'peared to be giving the orders was a big feller with black whiskers. I didn't hardly notice the others." Slade nodded again, and rolled him a cigarette on which he puffed gratefully.

"Now stretch out and rest for a little while I clean up things a bit," the ranger told him.

Picking up the dead guard's heavy body, seemingly without effort, he placed it inside the coach with the other, making room for the driver to lie in comfort. He waited a few more minutes, then assisted the driver to enter the coach. With a word to Shadow, he mounted to the driver's seat and headed the coach and its grim burden to town, the big black ambling along sedately after the equipage.

The splendor of the sunset was flaming the sky when they reached El Paso, to immediately attract the attention of people on the streets.

"Find Doc McChesney and the sheriff and tell them to hurry to the stage station," Slade called. Men darted off to care for the matter.

When he pulled to a halt in front of the station, there was at once turmoil. Slade checked it and issued orders.

"Take care of the horses," he told the bewildered manager. "Leave the coach where it is until Doc has a look at the driver. I'll tell you what happened, so far as I know, as soon as the sheriff arrives. Don't allow anybody to approach the driver in the coach. I suppose the stage was packing money today?"

"It was, plenty," the manager replied. "To hell with it! We are insured. But, my God! Those poor guards, and the driver!"

"I think the driver will be okay, but there's nothing to do about the guards save give them a decent burial," Slade said. The manager bowed his head, with muttering lips.

"Anything I can do for you, Mr. Slade?" he asked when his prayer for repose of the dead was finished.

"I could stand a cup of coffee," Slade answered.

"Have it right away," promised the manager, and wasted no time making good.

While Slade was drinking his coffee, Doc McChesney arrived, glanced at the wounded driver.

"Okay, somebody give me a hand and we'll take him in the station and put him in a chair so I can give him a once-over," he said. "No bones broken, Walt? That's good. I'll give him a stimulant and change the pads. See you've taken care of him okay. Lucky you came along, though. Otherwise he would have bled to death. As it is, he'll be rarin' to go in a week or so."

Sheriff Serby put in an appearance, and Slade recounted what the driver told him of the incident. Serby shot him a meaningful glance.

"And you figure it was—"

"Of course," Slade interrupted. "He was the big fellow with the beard the driver saw. We'll have a little talk later. Right now I feel the need for a surrounding, and I want to take care of my horse."

With the thanks of the manager following him, Slade and the sheriff set out for Roony's, pausing at Shadow's stable to make sure all his wants would be taken care of. Doc had dispatched a couple of stage employees to fetch a stretcher from his office, planning to convey the driver there and keep him overnight so he could keep an eye on him.

"I spotted one of Gordo's *amigos* in the crowd at the station," Slade remarked as they entered the restaurant. "He heard all that was said. I gave him the nod and he headed for Pablo's *cantina* to let them know that everything is okay."

"A good notion," said the sheriff. "Expect the little gal was worried. Say, not many guzzlers here. Early, though; they'll be staggerin' in 'fore long. Hello, Roony, we crave nourishment."

"Coming up," replied Roony as he hustled to the kitchen. The sheriff glanced expectantly at Slade, who obliged by a detailed account of the day's discovery. Serby exclaimed his astonishment.

"You're the limit!" he growled. "The last thing anybody else would have thought of. So that's where those little bunches of cows are that Judson and Owen and the Bar A and others swear they've been losing and never able to track down. Combing the Huecos, watching the Rio Grande fords, and so forth, and never spotting a critter, while the hellions build up a nice herd in that canyon and then shove 'em across to the New Mexico buyers. Holy hoppin' horn toads! And you figure the sidewinders have a hole-up in that canyon?"

"I'm positive they have," Slade replied. "The smell of stale wood smoke is pronounced, with no indications of fires having been kindled. Which means that somehow the fires have been kept under cover."

"Any notion where it is?"

"A vague one, that I hope to put to the test," Slade answered. "Another thing so obvious that the casual observer is likely to overlook it for that very reason."

"But as it happens, *El Halcón* is not a casual observer," the sheriff said. "Guess the devil is well-heeled after that big haul today; it was plenty. Think he might lay off for a while now?"

"Perhaps," Slade conceded. "I haven't made up my mind as to that."

"Why did they ride east?" wondered Serby. "You'd think they would have headed for the Franklins, if they have their hole-up there."

"Just between you and me, I'm glad they didn't," Slade answered. "If they had, the chances are I'd have barged into them head-on, and odds of four to one on an open trail are just a mite too lopsided for comfort. As to why they rode east? Perhaps Gaunt knew the driver wasn't dead, didn't realize how badly hurt he was, and wanted him to see them ride east and so report it. Also, the shrewd devil knew that no matter which way they rode, they had to cross open prairie and there was no telling who might spot them. Well, here comes our chuck and it looks prime."

"And let's get on the outside of it before we collapse," said Serby. "I'm as empty as a rumhole keeper's head."

Roony, for whom the slander was intended, did not deign to reply.

The place was filling up with people excitingly discussing the stage robbery, marveling at the ingenuity displayed by the outlaws. The sheriff chuckled.

"Some of them are saying if you'd just gotten there a little sooner they wouldn't have gotten away with it," he remarked.

"Their confidence is inspiring, but if I'd arrived on the scene a little sooner, I would have very likely been ending up one of the victims," Slade smiled.

"I doubt it," said Serby.

"I'm thankful nobody appears to be wondering what I was doing up there," Slade observed. "I hope the same goes for Gaunt, for it is essential that I somehow discover that hole-up, and if he realizes I was in the canyon today, I might find myself riding into a nice trap. Well, that's a chance I'll have to take."

"Going it alone?"

"I think it will be best," Slade decided. "On such an expedition, one is less liable to be spotted than several. I really don't anticipate any trouble, the way I plan to work it. But if I am successful in my little voyage of discovery, when you and I and Gordo ride that way, it will be a different matter."

"The sooner the better," growled Serby. "I'm sure fed up with that sidewinder and itching to line sights with him. Do you figure the three hellions that helped him rob the stage are all of his bunch left?"

"I'm of that opinion," Slade replied. "Well, suppose we amble down to Pablo's *cantina* for a while. Don't figure on any more excitement tonight."

There wasn't, but the following night, some three hours after full dark found Slade again riding north by east, again carefully studying the back track with care before crossing the north trail and swinging west to the narrow canyon in the Franklins.

Without incident of any sort, he reached the canyon mouth. This time, however, he did not enter but rode up the slope that paralleled it on the east. Topping the crest, he continued along the rocky lip until, shortly, he came to where the steep end wall boxed the gorge. The bright starlight showed that nearby a little spring bubbled up through the loam and that the ground was carpeted with grass.

"So I guess you can make out while I go about

my little chore of cliff-climbing or descending," he told Shadow as he flipped out the bit and loosened the cinches, allowing the horse to graze and drink in comfort. Then he tackled the box wall of the canyon.

Twenty

AS SLADE EXPECTED, there were knobs of stone, shallow ledges, and crevices that provided hand-holds. Also the stout creepers helped. The descent, while not easy, was not seriously difficult, although there were places where a slip would have been fatal. But *El Halcón*, experienced in rock work, made none. Without mishap he reached the canyon floor, close to the west-side wall and behind the mat of vines and creepers. Exultantly he saw, although the light was dim, that men and horses had recently passed that way, there being plenty of room between the cliff face and the trailing creepers to accommodate both.

For long minutes he stood motionless, peering and listening, arriving at the conclusion that there was nobody anywhere near. He began to cautiously creep along behind the vines, hugging the rock wall, knowing that were some of the outlaws around, he might find himself on a very hot spot indeed.

But the silence remained unbroken, no signs of movement. He had covered perhaps a quarter of the width of the canyon when he came to what he had been confident he would find. A dark opening split the face of the cliff—the mouth of a cave, so screened by the vines and creepers as to be invisible from the canyon floor.

Again he paused to listen, then glided into the passage. From his pocket he drew a candle and touched a match to the wick. The little flame showed he was in a rock walled and ceiled passage a dozen feet or so in width and a little more in height. After a moment's hesitancy, he moved ahead. Half a dozen yards or so and the passage abruptly widened and he found himself in a room perhaps a score and a half feet square, the narrower passage continuing through the far wall.

The room showed plenty of signs of prolonged occupancy. There were bunks built against the walls, a roughly constructed table and chairs. There was a stone fireplace, with a crevice above it to care for the smoke, cooking utensils scattered about. On shelves pegged to one wall was a store of staple provisions. Over to one side the horses had been bedded down. Several rifles stood in a corner. All in all, quite a cosy hangout where the outlaws could lie low in comfort did they think it advisable to do so for a spell, or gather to plan a depredation. And right in El Paso's back yard! Slade's admiration for Herman Gaunt's ingenuity increased.

He glanced around again, decided to explore the continuation of the passage through the far wall.

The moment he entered the narrow natural tunnel, he realized there was a strong down-draft; evidently somewhere ahead was an opening to the outer air. Which might prove interesting.

He had covered some fifty feet or so when he abruptly halted. The candle flicker showed he was standing on the edge of a chasm that split the passage floor from side to side. From far, far below came a faint murmur of running water. Holding the candle high, he endeavored to plumb the depths of the chasm without success. However he did see that the awful hole did not extend quite from wall to wall of the passage. To the left, a crumbly-looking ledge little more than a foot wide hugged the wall, extending into the darkness.

"Well, guess we've gone as far as we are going," he told the candle. "Sure for certain I don't intend to risk creeping along that thread of very uncertain-looking stone."

But man proposes, fate disposes. He was just turning back the way he had come when his keen ears caught a sound that stopped him dead in his tracks, snuffing out the candle, a sound of voices. The outlaws were coming in the "front" door. He was trapped!

El Halcón found himself in a very unpleasant position. Did one follow the passage to dispose of stable sweepings or other garbage, the chasm undoubtedly being the depository of refuse, he could not hope to remain undiscovered, with the odds devilishly against him. Only one thing to do, risk the highly dangerous-looking ledge. He glided to the side wall, feeling his way in the black dark, stepped onto the crumbly surface of the ledge and began inching his way along it. Behind him the sound of voices loudened, and gruff laughter and a rattling of cooking utensils. Sounded like the hellions were preparing for a lengthy sojourn in the hideout. He continued to ease along the ledge, his breath catching in his throat as the uncertain surface yielded to the pressure of his boots. Sweat started out on his temples as a foot slid over the crumbly edge and only a miracle of agility enabled him to regain his balance and saved him from plunging into the gulf. And there was always the frightening possibility that the ledge would peter out before reaching the far side of the chasm, and it was highly doubtful he could turn on the narrow shelf to retrace his steps.

However, it didn't. With a deep breath of relief, he felt the solid floor of the tunnel which had developed a sharp upward slant, beneath his feet.

And not a moment too soon. Behind, the voices loudened and there was a rattling and banging and a flicker of light. Slade plunged ahead, nor did he slacken his speed until he was yards up the slanting bore.

Quickly another problem began obtruding. The passage was narrowing more and more. Looked like the opening, wherever the devil it was, might well be too small for him to worm through. However, fate apparently decided to take a hand again. A crumbling of earth, a breath of cool fresh air, and he was out, sprawling on the ground for several minutes to recover from his nerve-racking experience.

Overhead, the stars shone brightly in a clear sky, providing enough light for him to see that he was no great distance from where he left his horse. Another brief period and he had flipped the bit back into place, tightened the cinches, and was heading for El Paso at a fast pace.

It was close to daylight when Slade arrived in town, but he found the sheriff in Roony's awaiting him. He listened with absorbed interest to *El Halcón*'s account of the night's adventures, shook his head and swore.

"A pity we weren't all there," he grumbled. "Woulda been a good chance to get the drop on the hellions."

"And what would have been the charge against them?" Slade countered. "No law against folks holing up in a cave. No, we still have to get the devils dead to rights. Anyhow, we know where to look for them if they do pull something, which helps. Well, I'm going to call it a night. Still haven't got over that creep along the wall with a few hundred feet of nothing reaching up for me."

When Slade entered the sheriff's office the following afternoon, there was a visitor awaiting him. A youngish man with a lean face, thin, tight lips and hard, watchful eyes.

It was John Cradlebaugh, his Land Office friend, and the Land Office trouble-shooter. They shook hands with warmth, and after a session of reminiscing over coffee and cigarettes, the sheriff secured a horse for Cradlebaugh and all three rode to where the break in the river bank occurred. Cradlebaugh looked the situation over with the eye of experience.

"You are absolutely right, Walt, per usual, in your deductions and conclusions," he said. "I am ready to verify them. The change in the river's course was undoubtedly man-made. When you are ready to do so, you can assure your farmer friends down there that their titles are secure and the land is still a part of Mexico. An amazingly clever stunt, changing the flow that way. The devil who did it is a genius of a high order. As you figured, there's a good chance that he got his inspiration from Cordova Island in El Paso. Yes, one of the most outstanding pieces of skulduggery I ever encountered, and I've encountered plenty in my time. Okay, this angle is taken care of. Go ahead and twirl your loop."

"As soon as I can decide where to make my throw," Slade replied, with a rather wry smile. "So far a suitable opportunity hasn't presented."

"You'll make one, sooner or later," Cradlebaugh predicted cheerfully.

"You're darn right," agreed the sheriff. "Let's go eat."

Cradlebaugh chuckled hugely over Slade's account of his adventure in the cave.

"You can get yourself into the darndest predicaments," he said. "Wonder why those devils were getting together there?"

"Seeing as we have had no reports of a depredation anywhere, I'd say it was to plan something," was Slade's guess.

The night passed peacefully. Cradlebaugh caught a train east the following morning, after again congratulating Slade on his acumen.

"Write and let me know how it went, after you finish the chore," he requested. Slade promised to do so.

The day also passed peacefully, as did the night that followed, and the next day, with Slade growing acutely uneasy.

"The hellion is building up something, I'll swear to it," he declared. "What? I haven't a ghost of an idea. We'll just have to wait and hold ourselves ready for anything." The sheriff swore wearily and stuffed his pipe.

And then, shortly after full dark, Gordo

Allendes came hurrying into the office, his eyes snapping.

"*Capitán*," he said, "as you ordered, two *amigos* have the close watch over the *Señor* Wilfred, the owner of the Arcadia *cantina*, kept. This night he from the *cantina* rode. North he rode to the trail. From the growth rode the *ladrone* Gaunt and three others. With guns they held they menaced the *Señor* Wilfred. His gun they took. Then, he by them surrounded, they rode on north across the trail."

"What in blazes!" exclaimed the sheriff.

"In my opinion, Gaunt caught on that Wilfred recognized him and plans to rid himself of such a menace, although he may have something additional in mind," Slade said as he surged to his feet. "Got your horse handy, Gordo?"

"At the rack he stands," the knifeman answered.

"Okay," Slade said. "We ride, and perhaps we can save Wilfred. How are you at rock work, Trevis?"

"Not bad," the sheriff replied. "Did a lot of it when I was younger. Cliffs and holes in the ground always held a fascination for me. You figure they aim to take Wilfred to the hole-up in the cave? Why would they do that?"

"A perfect spot to dispose of his body, down that chasm," Slade said grimly. "Let's go! How about you when it comes to cliff scrambling, Gordo?"

"Where *Capitán* leads, I follow," the knifeman returned composedly. Slade chuckled, and led the way to the stable. As they rode north, he said, "The first time I rode this way, I figured a short cut that I believe will allow us to get to the hangout ahead of the devils, which I earnestly wish to do. They may not wait long to dispose of their victim once they feel secure, although I wouldn't put it past the sadistic devil to go in for a little torturing first."

As he spoke, from a cunningly concealed secret pocket in his broad leather belt he drew the famous silver star set on a silver circle, the feared and honored badge of the Texas Rangers, glanced at it, then returned it to its hiding place.

"A notion I can still get by as a deputy sheriff and stay undercover in the section for a while longer," he explained.

"You can," the sheriff stated positively.

Now Slade quickened the pace, following the short cut of which he spoke. Reaching the slope paralleling the canyon, he called a halt and for some little time sat studying the terrain.

"I believe we are ahead of them," he finally said, "Hope so, for if they happen to come along and spot us going up the slope, the advantage will all be theirs."

However, fate, or something, was their friend and they reached the crest with nothing happening. The horses were quickly cared for and

218

they tackled the cliff. Slade was pleased to see that the descent posed no great hazard for the tough old sheriff. Reaching the canyon floor, screened by the vines and creepers, Slade again called a halt and stood peering and listening. No sound broke the great hush of the wastelands, and no gleam of light played on the creepers outside the cave mouth.

"I'm pretty sure we're ahead of them," Slade breathed. "If I'm mistaken and they're holed up waiting for us, I figure we'll find it out soon enough." He did not need to mention that if he was mistaken, the first notification of the fact would very probably be a blast of gunfire they would see but wouldn't hear, lead travelling a bit faster than sound. He eased ahead, paused again at the cave mouth. Still no sound broke the silence, and if there was somebody inside the cave, he believed he would have heard their breathing. He clasped the sheriff's hand.

"Take hold of Gordo's and don't let go of mine," he whispered. "Here we go."

Drawing a deep breath, he entered the cave. Nothing happened. With his uncanny sense of distance and direction, he led his companions across the room to the narrowed passage in the far wall, and on into it almost to the chasm.

"So far, so good," he said in low tones. "Now all we can do is await developments."

The wait was not too long. A clatter of horses' irons sounded on the rock floor, and voices. A light flared up. Saddle leather creaked and popped as riders dismounted.

"All right, Wilfred, sit down at the table, with your hands on it in front of you," said a voice, Herman Gaunt's. "That's right. I have all the papers ready for you to sign. Bert, heat the poker, good and hot."

Followed sounds of a fire being kindled. Slade had no idea what it was all about, but he felt it was time to act. "You do the talking, Trevis," he breathed into the sheriff's ear. "We must give them a chance to surrender. They won't. So shoot fast and shoot straight." He glided toward the lighted room, the others crowding alongside him. His glance swept the scene before them.

Chet Wilfred, his face ashen, his eyes wild, sat at the table. Beside him, Herman Gaunt riffled a handful of papers. The other three outlaws were busy at the fireplace. As the posse stepped into view, the sheriff's voice rang out,

"Up! You're covered and under arrest. In the name of the law!"

A chorus of startled exclamations. The outlaws at the fireplace leaped erect and whirled toward the sound of his voice. Herman Gaunt reached with his usual instant grasp of opportunity. He seized Wilfred and jerked him to his feet, holding him as a shield. His gun blazed over Wilfred's shoulder, the slug fanning the ducking ranger's face.

El Halcón knew he had to take a terrible chance. Barely half of Gaunt's face was visible, almost in line with Wilfred's, who was lurching and struggling, but helpless in Gaunt's iron grip. His breath tight in his throat, Slade fired.

Gaunt's one glittering eye Slade could see went blank; blood spurted. The outlaw chief reeled back with a horrible gasping scream, and fell. Wilfred, off-balance, slumped beside his dead body.

Gordo and the sheriff were shooting it out with the remaining three owlhoots. Slade's booming Colts joined in. Caught completely off-balance, in the glare of the bracket lamps and the fire, the posse in the shadow, the outlaws never had a chance. Another moment and there were four motionless forms on the floor of the cave.

"And that takes care of that," Slade said in a tired voice as he reloaded his Colts.

Wilfred scrambled to his feet. "My God, but I'm glad to see you fellows," he said fervently. "I figured I was a goner for sure. Guess I would have been were it not for you."

"What are those papers Gaunt ordered you to sign?" Slade asked.

"Bills of sale and deeds to my saloon, the Arcadia, and the *cantina* in Juarez I recently purchased," Wilfred replied. "If I refused to sign, he intended to burn my eyes out with that poker the devils were heating."

"Nice people!" growled the sheriff.

Slade glanced around. "Well, we have horses saddled and bridled we can use to get out of the canyon and up the slope to our own cayuses, unless you'd prefer to tackle that cliff again, Trevis," he said.

"Never mind the blankety-blank cliff," retorted Serby. "Let's get the heck outa here. Pick up the carcasses tomorrow; they won't walk away."

The trip back to town was uneventful, and everybody called it a night without recounting what had happened. There was plenty of excitement and comment when the bodies were brought in and Hermant Gaunt's duplicity revealed. Slade rode to the farmlands with the good news for the farmers that their titles were secure. Both he and the news were received with grateful enthusiasm. That night he and the sheriff sat in the *cantina* with Carmen, Gordo, and Pablo and talked things over.

"Suppose you'll be ambling now, eh?" Serby remarked.

"Not just yet," Slade replied smilingly "There's still another rose bush I have to see burst into bloom."

Pablo and the sheriff roared with laughter; Gordo grinned. Carmen blushed.

Several days later she said goodbye with a

smile, but with her beautiful eyes wistful as she watched him ride away, tall and graceful atop his great black horse, to where duty called and new adventure waited.

Center Point Large Print
600 Brooks Road / PO Box 1
Thorndike, ME 04986-0001 USA

(207) 568-3717

US & Canada:
1 800 929-9108
www.centerpointlargeprint.com